"Emily, _____."

"Because you l_____ ___r voice was not w_____

"And because I ___ ___. And because I think you like me. I understand that you haven't really thought about marrying again. We've already had passion, Emily. You with your husband, and me with Julia. What you and I have is a pleasant friendship—a great friendship, actually—with the children to give us even more in common. Then, in the future, if the both of us want it—maybe we could have a real marriage. But for now, isn't half a loaf better than none?"

"If both of us want it," Emily repeated, her head reeling. So much for any thoughts of romance.

But, oh, how she wanted some romance!

Dear Reader,

During this holiday season, as friends and loved ones gather for Thanksgiving, Silhouette Romance is celebrating all the joys of family and, of course, romance!

Each month in 1992, as part of our WRITTEN IN THE STARS series, we're proud to present a Silhouette Romance that focuses on the hero and his astrological sign. This month we're featuring sexy Scorpio Luke Manning. You may remember Luke as the jilted fiancé from Kasey Michaels's *Lion on the Prowl.* In *Prenuptial Agreement,* Luke finds true love . . . right in his own backyard.

We have an extra reason to celebrate this month—Stella Bagwell's HEARTLAND HOLIDAYS trilogy. In *Their First Thanksgiving,* Sam Gallagher meets his match when Olivia Westcott returns to the family's Arkansas farm. She'd turned down Sam's proposal once, but he wasn't about to let her go this time.

To round out the month we have warm, wonderful love stories from Anne Peters, Kate Bradley, Patti Standard—and another heart-stopping cowboy from Dorsey Kelley.

In the months to come, watch for Silhouette Romance novels by many more of your favorite authors, including Diana Palmer, Annette Broadrick, Elizabeth August and Marie Ferrarella.

The Silhouette authors and editors love to hear from readers, and we'd love to hear from *you.*

Happy reading from all of us at Silhouette!

Valerie Susan Hayward
Senior Editor

PRENUPTIAL AGREEMENT
Kasey Michaels

Silhouette
ROMANCE™
Published by Silhouette Books New York
America's Publisher of Contemporary Romance

To my new editor, Valerie Hayward, a kindred spirit, and to the memory of that wonderful New York City lunch when we sat for hours and talked about everything "under the sun"!

SILHOUETTE BOOKS
300 E. 42nd St., New York, N.Y. 10017

PRENUPTIAL AGREEMENT

Copyright © 1992 by Kasey Michaels

LOVE AND THE SCORPIO MAN
Copyright © 1992 by Harlequin Enterprises B.V.

ISBN: 0-373-08898-1

First Silhouette Books printing November 1992

Printed in the U.S.A.

KASEY MICHAELS

I am a Scorpio, but before anyone starts cracking jokes about my "passionate" sign, I want to tell you that the color red, an interest in things medical, dogged loyalty and a passionate nature are only four characteristics of a true Scorpio. We are usually secretive about matters closest to us, and in *Prenuptial Agreement,* I decided to write about another, less known Scorpion characteristic—our often misunderstood vulnerability. Yep, we're vulnerable. And when hurt, we retract into ourselves to make darned sure we aren't ever hurt in the same way again. We don't show our pain, but we feel it, deeply.

Luke Manning, my Scorpion hero, shows the imprint of his sign by becoming a pediatric surgeon. And after being disappointed in love, he reacts in true Scorpio form by retreating from that emotion with a firm conviction *never* to be hurt again.

I thought you might like to see what happens to these best-laid protective plans of one Scorpio male when his passionate nature cries foul!

SCORPIO

Eighth sign of the Zodiac
October 23 to November 22
Symbol: Scorpion
Planet: Mars and Pluto
Element: Water
Stone: Bloodstone, Topaz
Color: Dark red
Metal: Steel
Flower: Chrysanthemum
Lucky Day: Tuesday
Countries: Morocco, Norway
Cities: New Orleans, Liverpool, Baltimore

Famous Scorpios

Prince Charles
Richard Burton
Walter Cronkite
Dwight Yoakam

Katharine Hepburn
Grace Kelly
Georgia O'Keeffe
Vivien Leigh

★

Chapter One

SCORPIO: Opposite sex considers you attractive. Get ready for some excitement; perhaps a new love entering your life. You've been making do too long with the status quo. It's time to lift yourself out of that comfortable rut! Remember: don't neglect social obligations. Money matters dominate early and late.

Luke Manning had glanced at the headlines, skimmed the editorial page and read the comics before refolding the morning newspaper and leaving it behind on the kitchen table.

He had not read his horoscope. He never read his horoscope. He was a man of science, not one prone to take predictions based on his date of birth and the position of the stars to heart. Besides, how could anyone believe anything that was printed on the same page as their favorite comic strip?

"Good morn-ing, Doc-tor Man-ning."

Luke smiled in genuine pleasure as he heard the familiar high-pitched, singsong greeting and turned to see six-year-old Michael Cornell and his five-year-old sister, Sarah, standing on the wide concrete pavement that ran along the length of the row of mellowed brick town houses.

"And good morning to you, Michael and Sarah. Here you go," he said, locking the front door behind him before reaching into the pocket of his faded jeans to extract two nickels he had purposely put there before finishing off his coffee and heading out. Holding a coin in each hand, he offered them to the children. "Here's something else for your piggy banks."

Michael, his large brown eyes solemn, only shook his head. "Mommy says we can't take any more nickels, Dr. Manning. She says it's 'stor-shun'—or something like that."

Luke raised one well-defined eyebrow. "I think your mother meant *extortion*, Michael, although I don't believe talking to Fred through the fence to keep him happy can be considered extortion," he went on, referring to his friendly sheepdog, who unfortunately spent a lot of time confined in the backyard of Luke's house. "I'm sure you'd talk to Fred whether I gave you a nickel every day to do it or not. Isn't that right, Sarah?"

The child, whose full pink bottom lip had been thrust forward in a pout, nodded emphatically, causing her mop of blond curls to bob up and down around her chubby cheeks. "I love Fred," she pronounced gravely. "And he loves me, too! But Mommy says—"

"I know, Sarah," Luke interrupted, fearing the child might cry. "And mommies are always right. Tell you what, kids. I have a fairly light schedule today, so I should be home early. I'll have a talk with your mommy and daddy tonight when I get home from the hospital, and we'll see if we can arrange something, okay?"

"We don't have a daddy, Dr. Manning. He's dead. I never even seed him, but Mommy shows me pictures."

Luke winced as he belatedly remembered hearing somewhere that Mrs. Cornell had been widowed before Sarah had been born. "I'll bet they're great pictures too, honey. All right, I'll stop by tonight and talk to your mommy. But right now I've got to get moving or I'll be late."

"You gonna cut up another kid this morning, Dr. Manning?" Michael asked, his smile bloodthirsty, even if he was missing his top two front teeth.

Luke squatted in front of the child, taking hold of his arms. "Don't sound so thrilled, Michael. Yes, I am going into surgery this morning. But it isn't really cutting up people, you know. The children I operate on are sick, or have some problem that hurts them and makes them unhappy. I fix them up so they can be happy again and go out and play all day like you and Sarah. Understand?"

Michael frowned, then nodded. "Sure I do. You're a repairman, like the guy who came to fix our washing machine last week. Right?"

Luke sighed, smiling as he stood. Children were so literal. "Right, Michael, although I have to admit I never thought about it that way until you mentioned it. See you guys later."

"And you'll talk to Mommy tonight, Dr. Manning?" Michael called after Luke as he headed for his car. "Maybe she'll let you give us lollipops—the ones without sugar."

"Maybe," Luke agreed, waving goodbye before backing out of his parking space. He chuckled as he realized that the children appeared to have already figured everything out. If they couldn't have nickels, they'd take candy. It seemed fair. To a six-year-old.

Luke glanced at his watch as he pulled out of the small development of town houses and headed toward the hospital. He had left himself plenty of time to speak with the parents first before meeting his six-month-old patient in the operating room. He knew it wasn't strictly necessary to talk with them again. Everything had been explained yesterday, upon the child's admittance.

But Luke also knew that parents felt better when they had as much interaction with the surgeon as possible, if only so that they could judge whether or not he'd had a good night's sleep.

He never blamed parents for their anxieties or took offense at their sometimes pointed questions. Children were the most precious creatures in the universe, and he felt sure he would probably be ten times as nervous if any child of his ever had to go under the knife. After all, he had firsthand knowledge of all the things that could go wrong in an operating room.

Pulling his car into one of the Doctors Only parking spaces, Luke grabbed his attaché case and headed for the pediatric department, already mentally reviewing the first procedure he would perform that morning.

"Hi, Luke," one of his colleagues, Ben Easterly, greeted as Luke walked off the elevator onto the third floor. Ben, about to enter the elevator, held open the door, remarking, "We really have to stop meeting this way. Another big day at the office?"

"Two hernia repairs, a tonsillectomy and a badly broken tibia that will probably take me through lunch. You?"

"Healthy six-pound, four-ounce girl, delivered an hour ago," Ben answered, stripping off his green scrub cap. "Funny thing how in med school they never mentioned this little habit babies have of being born at the crack of dawn. I'm on my way home for a few hours of shut-eye before my afternoon office hours. I called Mary and she has breakfast waiting for me—among other things. Great institution, marriage, and I should know. You ought to try it, Luke. It might get you out of your rut."

Ben released the elevator door and it began to slide closed, blocking out the sight of his grinning face. "See ya!"

"Yeah, Ben, see ya," Luke called after him. "Everybody's a comedian," Luke murmured to the closed door, turning to head down the hallway toward the small office he maintained in the unit. On his way he passed by the nurses' station.

"Good morning, Dr. Manning. Lovely day, isn't it?"

"You're right on time, Dr. Manning. I always tell all the nurses—I can set my watch by your entrance in the mornings."

"I have your coffee ready, Dr. Manning. It's on your desk."

Luke thanked each of the women individually, from the head nurse down to the unit clerk, then closed the door of his office behind him, blocking out the rest of the world.

Throwing his attaché case onto the worn leather sofa that served as his bed more often than he'd like to admit, Luke picked up his coffee cup and walked to the window to look out at the wall that faced his office across a narrow, macadam courtyard, his view partially obscured by the steam that rose in a six-story-high cloud from the hospital laundry room in the basement.

The coffee was fresh and very hot, just like it was every morning. Seven days a week. Fifty-two weeks a year. The filled mug couldn't have been on his desk more than a few minutes.

I have your coffee ready, Dr. Manning.

I can set my watch by your entrance in the mornings.

Luke grimaced, turning away from the window. Good Lord—was he that predictable? He was only thirty-five. Could the nurse who'd said it be correct? Yes, he always came to the hospital early, if he didn't actually sleep here. Yes, he had worked every day of the past two years without a day off, without a vacation, without setting aside any time for himself.

Did that make him predictable?

Probably.

He didn't think he liked the term.

Great institution, marriage. You ought to try it, Luke. It might get you out of your rut.

Luke collapsed his long, lean frame into the chair behind his desk and ran a hand through his shaggy black hair, which would have been cut last week, except for that emergency appendectomy that had come up a half hour before his appointment. Ben hadn't meant anything by that crack about marriage. He was just being Ben.

Still, the remark had hurt.

Luke had nothing against marriage. In fact, two years ago he had been very much in love and engaged to be married. Ben knew that. Everyone knew that.

But the engagement hadn't worked out. Everyone knew that, too.

Sighing, Luke reached forward to pick up the heavily engraved invitation to the annual board of directors' dinner dance for physicians, which had been sitting on his desk for almost a week.

Invitation?

Command was more like it. *You have been invited! You will attend!*

Even worse, the invitation was addressed to "Dr. Luke Manning and Guest." He hadn't been out on a date in two years. Who was his guest supposed to be—Fred?

It wasn't as if Luke didn't know any women. He knew dozens, most of them nurses or doctors here at the hospital. Luke wasn't vain, but he would have to be unbelievably oblivious not to know he was considered to be the most eligible bachelor on staff at the hospital.

And that was the problem.

Tossing down the invitation, he leaned back in his chair, remembering something that had happened just yesterday.

"You're really wonderful with children, Doctor," one of the young, attractive floor nurses had said as he exited a patient's room. "All the children love you. You should have at least a dozen of your own." The nurse's tone, her smile and the provocative switch of her hips as she had walked away from him had added the unspoken message, "And I'd be more than happy to carry them for you."

He hadn't bothered to tell the nurse that, although he would like very much to have children of his own, he had yet to find the right woman. Especially since he hadn't been looking for her.

Not for two years. Not since Julia.

After his engagement was called off he had concentrated on his career, almost to the exclusion of everything and everyone else. His life revolved around the hospital, his patients, leaving him little time for personal involvement. And even less inclination to return to the dating jungle.

Luke sat forward once more, picking up the invitation, his gaze centering on the politely worded demand for a reply in the next two days. Last year he had cried off, pleading his work load, but he couldn't miss the dinner dance two years in a row.

Damn. He'd have to do something, and soon.

He looked toward his office door. It wasn't as if he couldn't find a date on his own. All he had to do was open that door and any of the nurses would volunteer to be his "and Guest."

Not that he planned to do anything so foolhardy. Luke wasn't looking for a date, or for a possible romance. All he wanted, all he needed, was a warm body on his arm for the night.

And no commitments.

Emily Cornell removed the plastic tray of microwavable brownies from the small oven, placed them on the counter and frowned. It just wasn't the same as made-from-scratch brownies. Oh, the enticing aroma was still there, but the looks? She wrinkled up her small nose in distaste.

Hardly appetizing.

She pushed at the top of the brownies with her fingertip, drawing it back quickly to suck on it; they were very hot. And lumpy looking. And sort of shriveled around the edges.

How Emily longed for the time to bake, using her own trusted recipes. How she longed to be able to put a roast on the table without first removing it from a freezer bag; and how she longed to have more time to read to Michael and Sarah instead of allowing them to amuse themselves with that idiot box called a television.

How she missed those quiet afternoons, with the children napping upstairs in their beds while she sewed their little clothes from patterns or hemmed a new set of curtains for the kitchen or just curled up and read a good book.

But such moments were luxuries not easily afforded and seldom indulged, and it had been that way since Mark had died. She had struggled to stay at home, but by the time Sarah was little more than a year old, Emily had been forced to go to work, enrolling the children at a local day-care center.

Leaving the tray of brownies to cool, she returned to the sink to finish loading the dishwasher.

It seemed strange to Emily. So many women wanted what she had—a house, children and a career—while all she longed for was the chance to stay home and be a full-time mother. Was that really too much to ask?

She bent to place the last pot in the dishwasher, then straightened once more, pushing a stray lock of shoulder-length sandy brown hair behind her ear as she looked out the window.

Emily sighed. They were gone—and she wasn't the least bit surprised. Michael and Sarah had promised to stay home, but once again that promise seemed to have been written on the wind. Removing her apron, she headed for the front door, passing through the small combination living and dining room.

She knew where to look, of course. They would be holding a vigil five doors down the street, Michael on his new bicycle and Sarah on her hand-me-down trike, both of them patiently waiting for Dr. Manning to come home. Ordinarily they would have been visiting

Dr. Manning's backyard, talking through the fence to that huge, strangely adorable sheepdog, except that Dr. Manning had promised to talk to her when he came home tonight.

Not that anything he had to say would change her mind. Oh, no. She might be a working mother, but she was still a mother. No stranger was going to give her children money. It just wasn't right. And that was exactly what she was going to tell him!

Emily paused for a moment to inspect her reflection in the mirror that hung in the small tiled foyer, knowing she would not be pleased by what she saw. She was right. Her hair was mussed, the dark circles she still had not been able to get used to seeing bruised the skin beneath her tired brown eyes, and her overall expression echoed that of nearly complete physical exhaustion.

She leaned forward to examine her complexion and frowned again. She could do what it said in all those women's magazines and go upstairs, give herself a facial—then, with cucumber slices on her eyes, lie down in a dark, quiet room. That is, she *could* do all that, if she had the time.

But she didn't.

She'd barely had time to wash her face and hands and change into shorts and an old pullover knit shirt after work, let alone give herself a beauty treatment.

And remember that article about it being possible to steal a half hour a day for a leisurely bubble bath to soothe away the tribulations of the day? What an impossible nirvana that was. The article *had* to have been meant as a joke. She hadn't had time for more than quick, early-morning showers since Mark died.

Maybe she ought to stop reading so many magazines, but what else was there to do on Saturday nights?

But enough self-pity. It didn't get anyone anywhere, did it? It certainly didn't get them a bubble bath! Taking a deep breath, Emily turned and put her hand on the doorknob, prepared—if not well armed—to go outside and do battle with the most-probably well-meaning but overly generous Dr. Manning.

The bell rang before she could open the door.

Emily's head spun sideways to take in the condition of the living area behind her. Her high heels were still in the foyer where she had stepped out of them, her purse lay open on the table below the mirror, her car keys beside it.

Michael's collection of miniature cars and a long, snaking orange plastic highway decorated the area in front of the loudly blaring television, with one orange ramp leading up to the badly flattened pillows on the worn couch.

Sarah's magnetic board and A-B-Cs were scattered on the dining-room table, along with an almost empty glass of milk the children must have missed when they had collected up the dinner dishes.

Emily's frown turned into a comic grimace of dismay. Obviously whoever had declared that a person had the upper hand if confrontations took place on their own turf had never seen her living room at seven o'clock at night!

The doorbell rang again, bringing her attention back to the moment she had been waiting for and dreading; the moment that was obviously at hand. After all, it couldn't be the papergirl, collecting for this week's service. She had come last night, just as everyone was sitting down to dinner.

And that's when Emily had discovered Michael and Sarah's "collection racket." She had been short of change, and Michael had offered to loan her some money from his "earnings."

She would have stormed down the street to confront Dr. Manning at that very moment, except his car had been gone and hadn't reappeared in his parking space before she had given up and tiredly crawled upstairs to bed a little after midnight.

Now, refusing to glance into the mirror again, which could only undermine her courage even more, Emily pinned a patently false smile to her face and pulled open the front door.

"Mrs. Cornell? Hi. My name is Luke Manning. I live down the street."

Emily fought the impulse to touch her fingers to her cheeks, hiding the circles beneath her eyes. She had seen Luke Manning before, several times, but always from a distance. She hadn't seen his smile up close before. Or his amazing, dark flashing eyes. Or noticed how his overly long black hair seemed to silently cry out to be smoothed by a woman's hand.

And he was tall. Taller than Mark; taller than she by nearly a foot. Lean, yet solid. Dependable looking. Trustworthy. Gentle yet strong. The sort of man a woman could lean on yet not feel smothered—the way she had felt smothered by Mark's overwhelming jealousy....

"Mrs. Cornell?"

"Oh, Lord!" Emily realized that she had been staring. Struggling for some sort of opening that wouldn't seem too harsh, she fell back on simple politeness and a garbled invitation. "Dr. Manning, forgive me. I—um—I just took some brownies out of the microwave and I, and I—"

Luke smiled down at her, his look effectively robbing her of the power of speech. "If that's an offer, Mrs. Cornell, I accept. I could smell them through your open window. I haven't had brownies in years."

Emily, recovering, pulled a face. "That's good. Then maybe you won't notice how they look." She stepped back from the door, motioning for him to follow. "If you'll come with me? The kitchen is this way."

He walked into the foyer, immediately dwarfing the small area while causing her throat to close, making it difficult for her to breathe, let alone speak.

"Yes, I know. All our houses have the same floor plan. By the way, Michael and Sarah asked me to tell you they will be at their Aunt Madge's, watching television."

Emily nodded. "That's Madge Sinclair, my neighbor. She watches them while I'm at work. Of course, Michael's in first grade now, so for most of the day she only has Sarah. The arrangement is so much better than the day-care center I used before we moved here. You'd think Madge would be sick of them by six o'clock, but—" They entered the kitchen, Emily swooping up the soiled apron to shove it behind the toaster, knowing she was talking too much. "Would you like some coffee with your brownie? It would have to be instant."

Her hands working without having to mentally force them to perform jobs they had done for years, Emily collected a dessert plate, knife, fork and napkin and quickly sliced a large hunk of brownie. She placed everything in front of Luke, who had cleared a spot at the cluttered kitchen table. He had moved Sarah's coloring books to one side and sat himself down, as if he felt comfortable in her house.

"You have any milk? I haven't had brownies and ice-cold milk since my mother died," he said, smiling at her.

That smile once again affected her physically in a way that told her she had better not try to eat any of the brownies, for fear she wouldn't be able to find her mouth without making a fool of herself.

Emily got him a tall glass of milk, then collapsed into a chair across the table from him, determined to remember that she had a bone to pick with this man. "Dr. Manning—"

He held up a hand, cutting her off. "Please, Mrs. Cornell, call me Luke. Office hours are over—and we are neighbors."

She nodded, swallowing hard, watching him eat. He really seemed to be enjoying the brownie. Imagine what he would do if he could taste one of her home-baked brownies! "Luke. Of course. And you should call me Emily, I suppose."

He popped the last bite of brownie in his mouth, followed up with the rest of the milk, then wiped his face with the thin, economy-priced paper napkin. "All right," he said as she rose to slice another large wedge of brownie for him. "'Emily-I-suppose' it is. Thank you," he said, accepting another brownie. "You're a great cook."

"Heat and serve isn't exactly my idea of cooking, Luke. I think maybe it's just that you've been too long without a brownie."

"You may be right. I've been eating hospital food and food that comes out of boxes for so long that I actually like some of it. Someday we can discuss the merits of heat-and-serve breakfasts. However, I guess that will have to wait. We ought to discuss this extortion business now."

Emily felt hot color running into her cheeks. Drat that Michael. Why did he always have to remember the wrong things? Did he ever close a door without slamming it, no matter how many times she reminded him? No, of course not. Had he ever remembered to floss his teeth before brushing without a half-dozen warnings about the dangers of plaque? In a pig's eye, he did!

But a word like *extortion,* carelessly uttered in exasperation—*that* little slip of the tongue had stuck in his mind like glue.

"Well, maybe not extortion, exactly—" she began nervously, only to sigh and say, "Okay, Luke. Extortion, even if the word sounds a little harsh. Think about it. They'll play with your dog if you pay them each a nickel a day. It's almost as if they have implied that they'd do something terrible to the dog if you didn't pay them. Besides, even though Michael and Sarah really like your dog, I don't want them to think they should accept gifts from strangers.''

''Absolutely!'' Luke agreed, rising. She craned her neck to watch as he carried the plate and glass over to the sink, then rinsed both under the tap. She had heard he was a surgeon. He certainly had the hands for it; long, straight fingers, square palms. His hands looked capable, yet almost beautiful.

And gentle. Very gentle.

''I came to the same conclusion myself,'' she heard him say, ''once I considered the implications. I guess I just didn't think that I was a stranger. Michael and Sarah have been the first faces I've seen every morning since you moved in last fall. Really, Emily, they're cute kids, saying good-morning, and holding out their hands to—''

''Whoa! Back up a minute here.'' Emily's eyes widened in disbelief and she hopped to her feet as her maternal intuition came racing to the fore, pushing thoughts about Luke's hands out of her mind. ''They've been taking nickels from you every day since we moved in? I don't believe it! And here I've spent most of last night and all day today rehearsing a speech to you about not leading little children on, letting them think they can be paid to be friends?'' She slapped a hand to her forehead. ''Why those miserable, money-grubbing little monsters. Next week they'll probably take their bikes downtown and start knocking over candy stores!''

Luke held up both his hands, those beautiful, ca-pable-looking hands, effectively silencing her once more. *Jelly.* She had been solid jelly ever since she'd opened the front door and seen his smile. "Whoa, yourself, Emily. I haven't been giving them nickels since last fall." Then he grinned. "I was giving them pennies. They asked for a raise last week."

Leaving Luke where he stood, her mind now mer-cifully clear of any notion that she had a wonderfully handsome doctor standing in her kitchen, Emily thrust her chin forward—the remainder of her body obliged to follow along behind—as she stomped toward the front door.

Luke was right on her heels. "What are you going to do, Emily?"

She tossed a fierce look over her shoulder and growled, "I'm going to murder them. *That's* what I'm going to do! Wanna watch?"

Chapter Two

JUNE 9:
YOUR DAILY ASTROLOGICAL FORECAST

SCORPIO: Cycle high. Obligations do not have to be chores if you plan for them. Be innovative. Why not take a chance? Who knows where it might lead.

Luke stepped off the elevator at precisely 7:30 a.m., still chuckling as`he remembered Michael and Sarah Cornell's greeting this morning—the one the children had delivered while standing with their hands very neatly tucked out of sight behind their backs.

Sarah, her blond curls confined in tight pigtails, her chubby child's body dressed in a pristine white cotton pullover and pink denim coveralls, had stood directly beside her brother, digging the toe of one pink sneaker into the concrete. She looked a lot like her mother, Sarah did, Luke remembered thinking at the time. She'd grow up to be a beautiful woman.

"Good morn-ing, Doc-tor Man-ning," they had chimed in unison, their tone more somber than joyful.

"Good morning, Michael and Sarah. How's it going today?"

The children had exchanged looks before Michael, his eyes nearly hidden behind a shock of sandy-colored hair exactly the same shade as Emily's, said, "Mommy says we're to 'pologize for what we did—and then give all the money back."

Michael's hands had come out from behind his back, and in his right hand was a much-crumpled ten-dollar bill. "Sarah and me already spent most of the money on candy and stuff when Aunt Madge took us along to the store, so Mommy loaned us this. We hafta do chores until we've paid her back. It'll take *forever!*"

"Very nearly, I suppose." Luke remembered doing his best to put a stern look on his face as he spoke, knowing he had failed miserably in the attempt. Leaning down, he had accepted the money. Emily, he knew, wouldn't allow him to take no for an answer. She was a great mother.

"But you know what, kids," he had offered, feeling himself to be more than fifty percent responsible for their predicament, "I think I might be able to help you out there. That is, if you want to do some chores for me, as well."

Sarah's eyes had begun to sparkle. "We can turn on the hose to give Fred water, and we can run up and down outside the fence so he can bark and get his exercise while he chases us," she said, jumping up and down so that her pigtails danced in the air.

Michael had joined in his sister's enthusiasm. "Can we start today, Dr. Manning? Can we? Can we?"

Before the children could get too excited, Luke had remembered that giving the children money without first gaining their mother's permission had been what had gotten them into this predicament in the first place. "I'll talk to your mother tonight when I get home, all right?"

Both had nodded their approval, their faces solemn. "That sounds like a good idea, Dr. Manning," Michael had agreed, slipping his arm around his sister's shoulders. "From now on we're going to ask Mommy about *everything* before we do it—right, Sarah?"

Luke had leaned down to ruffle the boy's hair. "Good thought, tiger," he said before telling them goodbye and heading for his car.

Now, a half hour later, he still remembered with pleasure the comical look of dismay the children had worn as he had closed his front door that morning to see them standing on the pavement, waiting for him.

Then he remembered Emily Cornell's face as she had crouched down in front of her children last night outside the Sinclair town house and earnestly explained that, although she loved them both very dearly, they had done a very bad thing.

He didn't know who looked more sorry, the children or their mother. She had appeared as woebegone, and nearly as young, as Michael and Sarah. It was almost as if she had taken their guilt upon herself, as if she had been partially to blame.

Luke frowned now as he had then, knowing he had been at fault as well, no matter how harmless his intentions had been.

He still felt himself to be at fault. It had to be difficult being a single mother. Emily had her hands full, without him causing her problems. If only there was some way he could make it up to her. He looked forward to the end of the day and the thought of seeing her again.

"Hi, Luke. You're looking your usually somber self this morning."

Luke turned to see Ben Easterly approaching, dressed in a dark suit, gleaming white shirt and yellow tie. "And you look like you're on your way to a business breakfast. Have I forgotten something? Is there a general staff meeting this morning?"

Ben shook his head. "No, thank God. That's next week. I'm not really on today—Jerry's taking my calls. I just stopped by to check on one of my patients. Mary and I are leaving for New York in a couple of minutes—she's got matinee tickets to some Broadway show. One of her friends was supposed to go with her but she had a last-minute change of plans and I was elected. Say—speaking of shows—'fess up. Are you going to make the command-performance dinner dance this year, or have you already planned to have another emergency that night? Or couldn't you find a date?"

A picture of Emily Cornell—tired, obviously overworked, yet endearingly beautiful—flashed unbidden into Luke's brain. Emily Cornell, whom he most definitely owed a favor. She probably hadn't been out dancing since her husband died. What he saw as a chore would look to her like a much-welcomed break from routine. There couldn't possibly be any other reason for what he was thinking, could there?

Certainly not.

"A date, Ben? Oh, ye of little faith," Luke heard himself scoff before his better judgment could shut off his mouth. "Of course I have a date."

Luke's frown returned once Ben had moved off down the corridor. Sure, he had a date.

Now all he had to do was ask her.

"A dinner dance? You want to take *me* to a dinner dance? Why?"

"Why not?" Luke answered with maddening male logic, following her into the living room.

He had shown up after dark, at least an hour after Michael and Sarah had given up any hope of seeing him that night and gone to bed—about a half hour after Emily had given up that same hope and gone down to the basement to get the laundry out of the dryer, folding it while she watched a rerun on television.

Only she hadn't folded the laundry. She had sat in the darkened living room alone, blocking out the sound of the laugh track on television, remembering how Luke Manning had looked as he had sat in her kitchen the night before.

It had been a long time since a man had been in her kitchen, a long time since she had served a man brownies and watched as his expression told her he was pleased. Such a simple thing, such a simple pleasure.

She had almost forgotten how much she enjoyed watching a man eat.

Now Emily lifted the basket of laundry from the seat of one of the chairs and sat down to begin folding towels and miniature pairs of underwear and white socks while staring at Luke as if he had just sprouted another head.

Was the man out of his mind? She had only met him yesterday, and already he wanted to take her to something as obviously important as his hospital's annual dinner dance?

She watched as Luke lowered his tall frame onto the couch, his black turtleneck and faded blue jeans making almost as much of an impression on her as did his piercing dark eyes. It would be extremely easy to cast the handsome doctor in the role of Prince Charming—especially as she suddenly felt much like Cinderella being asked to the ball.

Only she didn't have any friendly fairy godmother to rustle up a magnificent fairy-tale gown and a pair of delicate glass slippers for her. Or a hairdresser who could tame her overlong hair, or an arsenal of cosmetics to tackle the dark circles under her eyes, or...

"I don't know that I could find a baby-sitter," she said, knowing she was grasping at straws. Madge would be more than happy to watch Michael and Sarah. Emily just didn't know if she could stand listening to Madge's matchmaking schemes.

Her friend had only seen the two of them together last night, and already the woman had been humming snatches from "Oh, Promise Me" as Luke had walked away down the pavement.

"And I really don't believe I have a thing to wear," she said when Luke didn't speak, but just sat there, a small smile on his face, staring straight through her with those same wonderful dark eyes.

Of course, she remembered, there was that new gown that had come into the shop last week, the size four that she had tried on over her lunch hour, knowing she'd never have any reason to purchase it, but longing to feel the luxury of silk against her skin. With her twenty percent employee's discount and a few skipped lunches, it might be possible to—

"Look, Emily," Luke said, interrupting her musings, "I don't want you to take this the wrong way. This dinner dance is not something I want to do, it's something I *have* to do. I only thought, well—it suddenly occurred to me this morning that you might like a chance to get out of the house for an evening. Away from the kids, not that they aren't wonderful. The invitation was meant to be in the way of an apology for the trouble I've caused you."

Expectations Emily hadn't realized she'd raised went plummeting to the ground, landing at her feet with a dull thud. "I see," she said, seeing everything clearly. All too clearly. "You're out to kill two birds with one stone. Find a partner for the dinner dance and ease your conscience about what went on between you and the kids. Very neat."

Then she frowned as another thought hit her. "No, wait a minute. I don't see. You could have eased your conscience by sending me flowers. Why go to such extremes? Why the invitation?''

Luke ran a hand through his hair, making her palms itch to perform that gesture herself. She picked up another towel and folded it, carefully matching corners as if her work was to be inspected at some later date.

Luke rose, to stand towering over her in the small room. The room that hadn't seemed all that small to her until yesterday, when he had entered it for the first time. In fact, suddenly the whole house seemed too small, so that the air was scented with the aroma of his after-shave, and the atmosphere was charged with his barely leashed energy. She had never been more aware of a man in her life.

"I have a reason, Emily, although it's rather embarrassing. I don't have a date,'' he said shortly, sliding his surgeon's hands into his pockets. "I haven't had a date since my engagement was broken two years ago.''

She dropped the towel onto her lap, ruining its precision folds. "You were engaged? What happened? Oh! I'm sorry. I shouldn't have asked anything so personal.''

"That's all right. I don't mind answering. My engagement was broken because my fiancée's husband came back.'' Luke grinned, and Emily felt her heart melt. Why were men always most handsome when they were vulnerable? He looked like Michael when he woke in the middle of the night, disturbed by a dream. She thrilled in gathering Michael close into her arms at moments like that, soothing him, infusing him with a generous dose of compassion and love.

Emily averted her eyes, doubting that Luke would ever need to be gathered close and comforted, and took refuge in humor. "Really? Well, that would be an impediment, wouldn't it? You loved her very much." This last was not a question, but an instinctive conclusion.

"Very much," Luke agreed, his smile somewhat wistful and tugging at her heart. "But my timing stank. We had only been engaged for a week when her ex showed up. Only he wasn't really her ex. It seems the divorce hadn't gone through. Anyway, they soon realized that they never should have parted in the first place, and Julia very politely offered me back my ring. I accepted. We still exchange Christmas cards."

"How terribly civilized," Emily murmured, longing to seek out this unknown Julia and give her a piece of her mind.

Or thank her. *Stop it, Emily,* she admonished herself. *You mustn't think that way!*

Luke took his hands from his pockets and spread them wide, palms up. "I don't know that many women anymore, Emily, although I could ask one of the nurses to be my guest. But I don't want to get involved. I'm not ready. To tell you the truth, I don't know if I'll ever be ready."

Emily heard what he said and stored the words away in her mind, if not her heart.

Luke reached into the laundry basket, pulled out a large bath towel emblazoned with a terry cloth rendering of some super hero, and began to fold it, his movements practiced and economical—those of a man who had been taking care of himself for a long time.

"Anyway," he continued, "I met you yesterday and I thought maybe we could be friends, seeing as how we have Michael and Sarah in common. Then, this morning, I realized that it was silly for me to let my invitation go to waste when we could both enjoy the evening. I hear the band is very good. So, what do you say? Do you still want to go?"

Emily accepted the folded towel and added it to the growing pile beside her. She took a deep breath, then let it out slowly. "As friends."

"Right. As friends. No strings attached."

Emily nodded, then smiled, praying he wouldn't notice that the action was forced. "That's good, Luke. Because if you think I'm going to give you a nickel for taking me to this dinner dance you've got another think coming!"

Luke seemed to visibly relax, making her at last realize that he had been nervous. That comforted her. She liked that he had been apprehensive about inviting her to the dinner dance and that he now appeared able to relax in her presence.

But now that he seemed to have loosened up, she felt herself growing twice as nervous. She stood, loading the folded towels and other items back into the basket on top of the other laundry. "Um—would you like some iced tea, or something?"

Smiling, he followed her into the kitchen and she watched as his gaze traveled over the countertop. "I guess it was too much to hope for. The kids gobbled them all up, didn't they?"

"The brownies?" Emily questioned, knowing she had eaten the last one herself after Michael and Sarah had gone to bed tonight. It pained her to admit it, but they had been good. Not as good as hers, but tasty. "It will only take me a minute to make more. The microwave, remember?"

Luke smiled as she headed for the cabinet to take down a package of brownie mix. "Here we go—instant calories and all the preservatives and chemicals a person could hope for."

"That's all right, Emily," Luke said, sitting himself in the same chair he had occupied the night before. "I'm a surgeon, not an internist. We like to live dangerously."

"On the *cutting* edge?" she quipped, laughing at her own joke. She turned away to measure tap water into a cup. "Seriously, Luke, I know you're a surgeon, but I don't know your specialty." She looked at him over her shoulder. "Orthopedics?"

He shook his head. "Pediatric surgery. I limit my practice to kids eighteen and under. It keeps me busy. Sometimes too busy. Which reminds me of something, Emily. I noticed that Michael and Sarah weren't wearing protective helmets yesterday while they were on their bikes. You do have helmets for them, don't you?"

Emily sighed as she poured the brownie mix into its special plastic pan, then placed it in the microwave. "They have them," she said. "It's getting those two to wear them that presents a problem."

Luke looked at her intensely, as if measuring her ability to make her own children behave. "It's important that they wear those helmets. I ought to know. I've seen what can happen when they aren't worn. I'll talk to the kids for you if you like," he said, his tone so helpful that she found it difficult to take offense even though she had been handling Michael and Sarah on her own for nearly all their lives. Luke seemed to care about her kids. That was nice; to have someone else who cared.

She leaned back against the counter, waiting for the buzzer to go off, signaling that the brownies were done. "I guess you've encountered a lot in your practice, Luke. I don't know if I could stand to see children in pain."

"It isn't always easy," he said, his dark eyes unreadable, "but the good times outweigh the bad. I also get to see a lot of children smile. Believe me, Emily, those smiles make it all worthwhile."

Emily felt her throat tighten as she watched varying emotions flit across Luke's face. A doctor. A doctor who specialized in helping children. Luke Manning was not only handsome, he was a very nice man. And he wanted to be her friend.

She guessed she could live with that.

"So, Luke," she heard herself say, "how would you like a big glass of ice-cold milk with your brownies?"

Chapter Three

JUNE 18:
YOUR DAILY ASTROLOGICAL FORECAST

SCORPIO: All work makes Scorpio a dull sign. Di-
rect your passions into play, and you may begin to
discover hints of what you believed to have been ir-
recoverably lost. Be on the lookout for red, the pas-
sionate color of your sign.

Luke stood back from the operating table, totally exhausted, as the "floating" nurse looked up at the clock to announce the time that marked the end of the procedure.

Five hours. No wonder his legs felt like rubber. But two-year-old Jamie had been a trooper all through the surgery, and the prognosis for a full recovery was good. Now all Luke had to do was write up his post-op instructions, talk with the parents, visit his other patients on the floor and examine two new patients in his office.

Then he could race home, feed and exercise Fred, shower and push himself into his tuxedo in time to pick Emily up at six-thirty for the dinner dance.

Right. And if he only had a little more time he could solve that little problem of world hunger while he was at it.

He gave orders to the post-op nurse, met with Jamie's parents and peeked in on several patients before retreating to the surgeons' lounge, gratefully sinking into one of the cracked leather chairs, wishing the day had another six hours in it.

Damn, he was tired. Beat. Worn-out. Bushed. Totally shot. But could he finish with his two new patients, go home, stick a frozen dinner in the microwave and curl up with those half-dozen medical journals he had been meaning to read?

No way.

He had to go dancing.

How had he gotten himself roped into this? He could have cried off from the dinner dance again this year. What was the board of directors going to do if he didn't attend? Shoot him?

Hardly.

If only Ben Easterly hadn't put his two cents in, jabbing at him about not having a date. If only he'd had the good sense to call an escort agency, if such things still existed or, failing that, a dating service.

But no. He had to have a flash of brilliance, didn't he? He had to remember Emily Cornell of the beautiful, sad, brown eyes—and that mess about giving her children money. He had to decide that he would pay her back for the trouble he'd caused by taking her to the dinner dance.

Stupid move, Manning. Stupid, stupid move. Why didn't you do as she suggested and buy her flowers? No. You had to ask her to go out dancing.

Dancing. He hadn't danced since that party at the country club two years ago when he and Julia—no! That was ancient history. Julia was married—had always been married, if he wanted to get technical about the thing. Max Rafferty was one hell of a nice guy. Together they had a great new baby son, Sean. He was happy for them all. Deliriously happy for them, actually.

Sure he was. Julia had Max, Max had Julia, they both had Sean—and he, Luke, had Fred.

Whoopee.

He levered himself out of the low-slung chair and headed for the coffee machine, catching a glimpse of his reflection in the small mirror that hung above the table. He leaned forward, looking at himself. Really looking at himself. And then he frowned.

What was wrong with this picture?

Luke shook his head as he answered his own question. It was simple really. What was wrong with this picture was that he was the only one in it.

Sometimes it seemed to Luke as if the whole world was married. The whole world had kids. The whole world, except for him, was happy.

He loved kids. He'd always loved kids. A man would *have* to love kids to become a pediatric surgeon. Either that or be crazy.

He also loved the institution of marriage. His parents had lived forty wonderful years together before they died in an automobile accident three Christmases ago. Once the shock of the sudden tragedy had passed, Luke had found comfort in the fact that neither of his parents had been forced to go on without the other. That's how close their married life had been. That was the example they had set for him.

And that was the sort of union he had envisioned with Julia. Not just a marriage, not just an exchange of rings and a shared bedroom, but a lifelong commitment to each other that transcended everything else life might bring to them.

Julia was gone and the dream had departed with her.

All Luke had left was the love and the dream, with no one to share either.

He didn't bother with the coffee, but picked up his scrub cap and headed for the shower room. He didn't have time for this. He had work to do.

And then he had to go dancing.

"Good eve-ning, Doc-tor Man-ning."

"Hi, kids. Your mom ready?" Luke smiled as he looked down on Michael and Sarah, their faces freshly scrubbed and shiny, their perfect little bodies already inserted into pajamas. They smelled of soap and clothes hung to dry in the sunshine, and they looked like innocent little angels.

But then looks were very often deceiving.

"Are you going to be my new daddy, Dr. Manning?" Sarah asked, tugging at his pants leg as he attempted to move past Emily's children to enter the living room.

He only smiled, mumbling something incoherent beneath his breath. He believed the word might have been *help!*

"Dr. Manning? What's a hunk? Aunt Madge says you're a real hunk, and Mommy shouldn't let you get away," Michael added while Luke tried to close his suddenly slack mouth.

Luke expelled air from his lungs in a rush, struggling to answer. After all, if he didn't, Michael would probably just ask again. Kids were like that. "A hunk is a sort of compliment women use to describe a man when they think he's handsome," he said, seating himself on the couch, just to have Sarah climb up beside him, flinging her chubby arms around his neck as she pressed her head against his shoulder.

Michael wrinkled up his nose in thought, then grimaced in a comical expression of dismay. "I'm the man of this family, Dr. Manning. Mommy told me so. Does that mean that I'm a hunk, too?" He stuck out his tongue. "I don't think I want to be a hunk. I hate girls, except for Sarah, and she doesn't count because she's my sister. Girls are yicky, and they try to kiss you!"

Luke laughed in spite of his effort to remain serious while speaking with the "man" of the Cornell family. "Them's the breaks, Michael. It's a burden all we handsome men have to bear. But I wouldn't worry about it too much if I were you. Someday you'll grow up and learn to like it."

Michael shook his head firmly. "When I grow up I'm going to be a fireman like my dad, and I'm never going to get married. That way, if I get burned up in a falling building nobody will have to cry because I don't come home anymore."

Luke had long ago ceased to be amazed by the heartbreaking candor of children, kids stricken with possibly terminal diseases who could speak so matter-of-factly about death and dying. But Michael's sudden admission shook him.

Sarah's arms tightened about his neck. "Mommy still cries once in a while, late at night. I hear her. She cried a whole lot when we had to leave our house in the country and move here. But Mommy said we couldn't afford it anymore."

Out of the mouths of babes. Five more minutes of this and Luke would know the entire Cornell family history. He didn't want to know. He didn't want to get involved, or at least not any more involved than he already was. He didn't want to think about Emily in tears, her haunting soft eyes clouded with pain.

His gaze darted around the living room nervously, looking for rescue from his thoughts.

"Isn't your Aunt Madge here, or are you going to her house?" he asked, trying to change the subject.

Michael hopped onto Luke's lap. "We're going to sleep at her house. All night. It was Aunt Madge's idea. Aunt Madge says opportunity only knocks once, or something like that."

Luke was beginning to feel as if he was choking, and it wasn't because Sarah still clung to him, the knot of his bow tie digging into his windpipe.

"Oh, look, Dr. Manning. Mommy's coming. Doesn't she look pretty?" Suddenly Luke was free, as Sarah, quickly followed by Michael, hopped down from the couch to race to the bottom of the steps.

Luke stood, ready to greet Emily—and more than ready to deposit Michael and Sarah with Madge Sinclair and escape to the relative safety of the country club. He took two steps forward, then looked up to see Emily slowly descending the stairs, one hand tightly clasping the rail.

Emily's shoulder-length sandy-colored hair had been swept up behind her left ear, to be held in place by a small rhinestone comb. Modest-length drop earrings also fashioned of rhinestones combined with the sophisticated hairstyle to draw attention to the smooth line of her chin and creamy shoulders.

Her large, soft brown eyes seemed somehow more defined, achingly youthful, although the only visible sign of makeup was the clear, matte red delineating her well-formed lips. He felt himself drawn to their color, their texture, their intriguing shape.

But it was her knee-length gown that caught and held his attention. Ivory in color, the gown was a close-fitting, off-the-shoulder style, fashioned in soft, touchable silk that seemed to whisper with every step she took.

The material making up the entire body of the gown had been set in one-inch horizontal pleats, so that it almost appeared as if Emily had been wrapped, mummylike, into it, while the short, off-the-shoulder sleeves were no more than poofs of dozens of ivory-colored petals that could just as easily have been feathers.

It was one hell of a gown. Demure, yet provocative. Classy, yet faintly decadent. Revealing, but oddly concealing. And very, very feminine.

Luke admired it on sight. During his courtship of Julia Sutherland, a dress designer, he had learned a lot about women's fashion. This gown, however, didn't look anything like one of her designs, even though it was made of one of Julia's favorite materials, silk. His ex-fiancée's designs were always extremely tailored, flowing and very attractive on tall, slim bodies.

Emily was not a tall woman, and she had mature curves rather than sleek lines and angles. Julia might have been able to wear this gown, for she was a beautiful woman, but Emily did more than wear it. She *was* the gown.

And she was all soft, touchable woman.

In short, Luke decided that he just might be in trouble.

He held out his arm so that Emily could take it as she descended the last few steps to stand in front of him. "You look wonderful," he heard himself say just as she turned away to listen to something Sarah had asked, so that he doubted she had heard him. He was rather glad, for he knew his voice had sounded somewhat strained. *No involvement, no involvement,* he chanted under his breath. *You don't want this, remember?*

"Yes, Sarah, of course you may touch it," Emily said, smiling down at the child who was holding out a hand to feel the ivory silk. "It's soft, isn't it?" she asked as Sarah laid her cheek against the material. "Just like the edges of your favorite blanket."

Luke heard Michael sniff and turned to see that the boy was looking at his mother strangely. "Where's your sweater, Mommy?" he asked. "You're gonna get cold going out like that."

Emily looked at Luke and he watched as a blush stole up from her creamy white shoulders, past the cinnamon sprinkle of freckles on her cheeks and nose, to travel all the way to the roots of her hair. "They— they aren't used to seeing me dressed up," she said, smiling at him before biting her bottom lip. "The last time I got dressed up it was to take them out on Halloween night, trick-or-treating."

"She went as a witch, with a mole on her nose and everything," Michael informed Luke. "She looked real neat that night. Not like now. You would have liked it."

"I'm sure I would have, Michael," Luke answered, careful to maintain a straight face as he looked at Emily. "Especially the mole."

Just then the doorbell rang and Sarah, who had been leaning against her mother's knee, began to cry. "I don't want you to go, Mommy. You've been gone all day."

Emily sighed and Luke saw her eyes fog with pain. "Oh, Sarah, darling," she said, going down on her knees in front of the child, "it's only this one night. Besides, Aunt Madge is already at the door, and you know she can't wait for you to come sleep at her house. She's already made up special little beds for you and Michael to sleep in. You can't disappoint her now."

Sarah's full bottom lip pushed out in a pout and a single tear coursed down one chubby cheek. "Will Aunt Madge make popcorn? Michael said maybe we could have popcorn while we watch television."

Emily was immediately on her feet, excusing herself as she headed for the kitchen. "I'll put a package in the microwave right now and you can take it over with you, okay? Now, Michael, answer the door and let Aunt Madge in."

Luke was left standing in the living room, feeling like the villain in some bad movie, bent on separating mother and child. And Emily was a mother, first and foremost, no matter how enticingly beautiful she appeared in her ivory gown. She had knelt on the floor, heedless of any damage Sarah might do to her dress. And she had left him without a backward look in order to make popcorn for the child before going to the country club for the biggest dinner dance of the year.

Yes, Emily was dedicated to her children, a real loving mother. Luke smiled to himself. He rather liked that in a woman. Maybe if he concentrated on how much he admired her as a mother he'd forget that she was a woman.

"Hello, Doctor Manning, nice to see you again."

He turned to see Madge Sinclair standing not ten feet from him, her smile oddly reminiscent of the cat that had just cornered the canary. "Hello, Mrs. Sinclair," he replied, suddenly on the defensive, remembering what Michael had said earlier. "Thank you for agreeing to watch the children for Emily."

Madge spread her hands wide as she tilted her head to one side, accepting his thanks as she would a hug. "It's the least I can do. Dear child. Working all day in that boutique, then coming home to two children and this entire big house to keep up. Frankly, I don't know how she does it. But she juggles it all beautifully. A born housewife and mother, that's what I tell Jim. That's my husband—Jim. Anyway, I tell Jim so all the time. I told him again just tonight, when I saw you walking up here in that nice tuxedo. I said, 'Jim, that Emily Cornell is a treasure, a real treasure. Someday she's going to make someone a very lucky, very happy man.' That's what I told him, Dr. Manning."

So much for forgetting Emily was a woman. Madge Sinclair wasn't about to let him forget that fact for a second. Luke cleared his throat. "I'm sure you did, Mrs. Sinclair." He knew it wasn't the most brilliant thing he might have said, but it was all he could think of while Madge Sinclair stood there sizing him up as if he were a prime cut of beef.

"Aunt Madge," Michael interrupted, "Mommy's making popcorn. She'll want us to floss our teeth after we eat popcorn."

Madge looked pointedly at Luke and rolled her eyes. "Such a good boy, but far too serious, don't you think, Dr. Manning? Needs a man's influence, you know. That's what I tell my Jim. I tell him, 'Jim, that boy needs a man's influence.' And do you know what my Jim says?"

Luke had a sneaking suspicion he knew *exactly* what Jim said, but he didn't volunteer. He didn't have to, for Madge quickly answered her own question.

" 'It isn't good for a boy to grow up without a father. Makes him think of dental floss instead of playing third base.' *That's* what my Jim said!'' she ended, crossing her arms in front of her ample chest as if daring him to refute her husband's words.

Luckily, Luke didn't have to say anything, for at that moment Emily reentered the living room and Madge immediately began to gush and carry on about how lovely Emily looked, "so youthful, so *bride-like.*"

It was Luke's turn to look away and roll his eyes. The woman was about as subtle as an inflamed appendix—and nearly as irritating, although Luke was sure she meant well.

"Ready?" Emily asked from somewhere behind him. "Madge is going to take the children upstairs to get their pillows, so we can leave now."

Luke heard the relief in her voice, as well as her anxiety, as she kissed the children good-night and told them to be good.

But at last, and none too soon for Luke's usually unflappable nerves, they were on the pavement and heading down the street to where he had parked his car. The sun was still hours above the horizon.

As he held open the door for Emily, he realized that, not only did she look wonderful, but she smelled good. Sort of a mixture of the clean, soap smell he had detected on the children and a light floral fragrance that put him in mind of green spring meadows dotted with wildflowers.

Mixed in there somewhere was a faint, appetizing hint of popcorn.

Madge had been right, Emily did look almost as young as her children. But her effect on him was not remotely reminiscent of the affection he felt for those children. For any child.

Especially, he thought as he levered himself behind the wheel and glanced over at her quickly, when he looked at her full red lips.

What did people talk about on dates?

On the drive to the country club they had exhausted the topics of the weather, the inconvenience caused by the resurfacing of their road last month and the merits of microwave popcorn. What was left?

She certainly didn't want to talk about politics or religion, two subjects she had been told were never to be discussed with casual acquaintances.

Standing at Luke's side, Emily took another sip of her cocktail, watching the other milling guests, anxious for dinner to be served. Maybe then they would be seated with some nice couple who had five children and she could "talk kids" with the wife.

Luke was a doctor. He couldn't want to hear about Michael's bout of chicken pox last spring and the way the pox on his left arm had seemed to make up a perfect outline of Italy, complete with Sicily. He must hear that kind of stuff all day long.

She peeked at him out of the corner of her eyes, watching as he nodded and smiled when an elderly gentleman named Baxter Something-or-other droned on and on to him about the proposed new nuclear-medicine wing at the hospital and the fact that it was going to cost "a bomb." Emily was confused, although she refused to admit it. To her anything nuclear was obviously a bomb.

Besides, Luke looked as bored as she was, so it didn't seem wise to ask any questions, thereby prolonging the man's one-sided conversation.

Emily shifted her wineglass into her other hand, wishing she had a napkin to wrap around it before the condensation on the outside of the glass dripped onto her new gown. Lord, but she felt naked. How long had it been since she'd worn anything this revealing? Her senior prom?

What had she and Mark talked about on their dates? They had started going together steadily when they were fourteen and she was in the ninth grade. They had talked about school and the chance his varsity football team might win the play-offs and about how they would get married when he had completed his second year of college, no matter what his parents said.

They had talked about themselves. *Their* lives, *their* plans, *their* love.

But she and Luke weren't a "them." They weren't a "we" or even an "us." They were just two people paired together for a single evening.

Friends.

Emily shivered slightly as Luke took a step backward and bumped against her. He smiled as he murmured an apology, then put his arm around her waist and drew her closer, saying something about not wanting to lose her in the crowd. She fought the urge to melt against him, extremely aware of his male body.

This accidental brushing together of their bodies caused her to panic again. How was she ever going to dance with him? She hadn't danced with anyone but Mark—except at their wedding, when she had danced with his father and the best man. Would she be able to follow his steps? Dear Lord, please don't let her stumble all over his feet!

She took another sip of wine, forced a smile, and ordered her mind to go blank.

After a few more minutes of listening to the economic gospel according to Baxter, the old man wandered away and she and Luke were left alone once more. Emily fought the urge to call him back.

As the silence between them grew, she stared into the bottom of her wineglass, wishing it contained crib notes on conducting polite conversation at cocktail parties.

"Are you having a good time?" Luke asked at last, waving to an acquaintance across the room. "Sorry about Baxter. He's on the board so I had to play nice. The man loves hearing the sound of his own voice."

Emily smiled and nodded, dying inside. A lock of hair had fallen onto Luke's forehead and she had to grip the wineglass with both hands in order to fight the urge to brush it back into place.

This was ridiculous! She shouldn't be feeling so tongue-tied. Luke had said they were friends. Okay. Friends it would be! So what did friends talk about?

Emily closed her eyes and sighed. Lord, she didn't have the faintest idea! She'd never had a male friend. For one thing, Mark wouldn't have allowed it.

"Sarah says Fred is a lovely dog," she heard herself say, and immediately longed to be able to dive headfirst into her wineglass.

Luke laughed. "That all depends on your opinion of shedding. There are days it looks like I have a shag rug in the kitchen—and it's a tile floor."

Emily smiled. What a dear man. He was trying to make this easier on her. She could tell. "Where did you come up with a name like Fred?"

Luke put a hand to her elbow, steering her into the dining room, as the guests had begun to move out of the area where the predinner cocktail hour had been held. "How? I'd like to tell you some clever story about how Fred came to be Fred, but there isn't any. The day I bought him I just lifted the hair away from his face and—well, he *looks* like a Fred."

"Flintstone or Mertz?"

"Fred Mertz from the old *I Love Lucy* show? Never him, Emily. Remember, that Fred was bald. So I guess that leaves Fred Flintstone, the cartoon caveman." Luke seemed to consider this for a moment, then shook his head. "No. Not him, either, although they both have enormous appetites. Now I've got it. Emily, have you ever shopped at that small grocery store on Cedar Crest Boulevard?"

"The butcher shop?"

Luke held out her chair for her at a round table that seated ten. "That's it. Fred looks just like the owner."

Emily waited until Luke had helped another woman with her chair and then taken his seat beside her. "But, Luke," she said, confused. "The owner's name is on the store. His name is William."

He laid his napkin on his lap, then turned to wink at her. "Yes, I know. But he *looks* like a Fred."

They both laughed at the shared joke before Luke introduced her to the other couples at the table.

Emily watched him as he made the introductions, giving her a small piece of information about each of them and referring to her quite naturally as his "good friend, Emily Cornell."

And that's when Emily knew that she had been worrying over nothing. The evening was going to turn out just fine.

This comfortable feeling lasted all the way through dinner—up until the moment the orchestra broke into its first song of the evening and Luke asked her to dance.

She waited until he had pulled out her chair for her, then walked toward the dance floor with all the eagerness of a condemned criminal being led to the gibbet.

Although the heels on her white kid shoes were high, she still felt she had to stand on tiptoe to rest her hand on Luke's shoulder. The action brought their bodies close together so that, even with her head averted as she affected a great interest in the other couples on the floor, she was aware of every inch of contact between them.

His fresh, clean breath feathered her hair. His slow even breathing, the rise and fall of his chest, sent tingles through her body. His hand, holding hers, seemed to burn into her palm.

As a matter of fact, she was so busy trying to fight off the effects of his closeness that it took her several seconds to realize that they were moving together flawlessly, as if they had been dancing with each other for years.

The thought caused her to stumble, stepping on his instep.

"Whoops," Luke said, holding her even more tightly as he swung her neatly into a turn, covering her misstep with the graceful maneuver. "Sorry about that, Emily. It's been a long time since I've done this. I guess I'm a little rusty."

Emily looked up at him and decided that if he wanted to take the blame, she might as well let him. After all, in a way, it was his fault. He didn't have to be so very handsome, did he? "That's all right, Luke," she answered sweetly, so that he squeezed her fingers.

"Having fun?" he asked, stepping into another graceful turn.

"I'm having a wonderful time, Luke," Emily responded politely, then realized that she wasn't just being polite. She was having a wonderful time. Perhaps the most wonderful time of her life. "Really, Luke."

"So am I, Emily," he told her, his dark eyes looking at her in a way that simultaneously pleased and puzzled her. She pressed her forehead against the lapel of his tuxedo and gave herself up to the music.

The song ended and Emily had to suppress a sigh as she made to step away from him and return to the table.

She had only taken two steps when the band began another song and Luke pulled her back into his arms.

They were the last couple to leave the dance floor when the band played "Good Night, Sweetheart" at midnight.

Chapter Four

Three months earlier, when Luke had arranged with another surgeon to cover for him on the Fourth of July holiday, he had thought he might take Fred and drive to the New Jersey shore, to visit with a distant cousin. Even three weeks ago the plan had still seemed a good one.

So, he wondered as he lay on the grass at Allentown's Lehigh Parkway—his head propped on one arm while an overly exuberant Fred pushed a rather wet ball into his face—how had he ended up here, not five miles from home?

The answer was simple. Michael and Sarah had invited him along on their picnic, and he just couldn't find it in his heart to refuse.

Just as he couldn't refuse when the children had invited him along two weeks ago when the three Cornells had gone to a newly opened pizza parlor near the Lehigh Valley Mall. There were games for the kids as well as a mechanized band of forest animals that sang and played banjos and drums a full ten decibels above "ridiculously loud."

Just as he had found himself inviting Emily and the children along for a day at Dorney Park's Wild Water Kingdom, using the children as an excuse so that he wouldn't feel so silly enjoying himself on the many twisting water rides.

Come to think of it, he'd been seeing a lot of Emily Cornell and her two children. Trips in his car to the local ice-cream parlor, evenings spent on hard bleachers watching six-year-old kids play baseball, even last Sunday afternoon when the children had helped him mow the lawn and Emily had made a big spaghetti supper for everyone. All sorts of domestic outings. And he had enjoyed every one of them.

Mostly he had enjoyed Emily's company. He felt comfortable with her, part of a family. It was a nice feeling.

He extracted the ball from Fred's jaws and tossed it in the general direction of the Little Lehigh River, hoping it would take the dog several minutes to find it, then lay back on the grass and looked at his surroundings.

He had liked Allentown the moment he had driven into the city limits on the way to be interviewed for his internship at one of the local hospitals. He'd come back to the city once he had completed his surgical residency in Philadelphia. Although it had been difficult to pass up the job offer from that Louisiana hospital, he had never wanted to leave Pennsylvania.

And he had never regretted his choice, he thought as he looked around at the rolling hills and the ages-old willow trees that lazily drooped along the banks of the small waterway. Even after his parents had died, freeing him to go anywhere he wished without worrying about their welfare, he had been content to stay put.

Turning onto his stomach, he looked out into the wide, open grassy area where Michael and Sarah were busily trying to play badminton without aid of either a net or any real measure of expertise. It looked as if they were having a good time, anyway.

Luke smiled as Sarah stuck out her tongue as she attempted to serve to Michael, her entire posture one of intense concentration. He liked these kids. Really liked them.

Oh, Sarah might cry just a little too easily, clinging to her mother, and Michael was more serious than a boy of six should be, but Emily was doing a fine job with them both. A very fine job.

And then there was Emily. They had come a long way since their first meeting, and the invitation to the dinner dance, he had decided long ago, had been a stroke of inspiration. He had enjoyed their conversation that night, and she had been like a feather in his arms on the dance floor. No. Not a feather. Feathers were beautiful to look at, but you couldn't dance with one, hold it in your arms, feel its softness against your body, breathe in its perfume—reminding yourself that you were alive.

Even Ben Easterly had been impressed with Emily, and everyone knew the guy was a self-appointed connoisseur of beautiful women, if not a particularly faithful one. Mary was his third wife.

Luke frowned, suddenly grateful that Ben hadn't seen Emily in her bathing suit. The man was entirely too observant for his own good and, after all, Emily was a single parent and totally available.

Luke had seen his share of single-parent families in the course of his practice, and his heart always went out to that parent, as well as to the children. Nature hadn't planned for children to have only one parent. It couldn't have, or it wouldn't take two to procreate.

Luke sat up, looking over to where Emily was busy setting out the plastic containers that held much of their lunch. She was dressed in a simple white blouse and navy blue shorts, her trim yet lush body lightly tanned by the sun. Her hair, usually left free to fall on her shoulders, had been tied up just behind her ears in a rubber band so that she looked no more than eighteen.

But the color staining her lips changed that impression, a light dashing of purest red that emphasized the lush fullness of her mouth. He really liked that red lipstick, having first noticed it the night of the dinner dance. Emily Cornell, both with and without ponytail, was a very attractive woman.

Refreshingly down-to-earth and easy to be with, she made no demands on him, didn't want to talk shop about the hospital and didn't make him feel he was under any pressure to deepen their association romantically. Yes, an altogether comfortable woman. Two years ago he'd been a victim of passion, unrequited passion at that, and rather believed he was happier without it now that it was over.

Yet when he was with Emily, when he saw her smile, or caught a whiff of her perfume, or watched her lips move as she talked—well, then he wondered if maybe, just perhaps, he wasn't as firm in his conviction as he had supposed himself to be. Maybe having a woman in his life again was just what he needed.

And maybe he'd better stop thinking this way. He and Emily were friends, nothing more. Good friends.

"Is the grill hot yet, Emily?" he asked, knowing that it was. He was a great fire builder, always had been. *Fire.* Emily's first husband had been a fireman. Her *first* husband? Now why in hell had he thought that? Maybe he'd been out in the sun too long?

"I can only count to 'two-one-thousand' with my hand an inch above the grate, so it must be ready," Emily answered, turning back to the wooden picnic table and shooing away a fly that had become too interested in the contents of one of the plastic containers. "I think you should put the steaks on now, Luke."

He obediently scrambled to his feet, dusting loose blades of grass from his khaki shorts, and walked over to the picnic table in time to receive the wrapped steaks from Emily. "Rare, or very rare, Emily? Take your pick."

She smiled, tilting her head to one side as if considering her options. "I think I'll take rare, thank you. Are you sure you want to be the chef? I can do it, if you'd rather rest. You didn't get in until very late last night." As soon as the words were out of her mouth she blushed, a reaction he had become familiar with over the last weeks, but one that still delighted him.

"And how would you know that, Ms. Cornell? No, don't tell me—Madge told you. After all, that woman seems to know everything and is more than happy to share it with the rest of us."

"Poor Madge. She means well. With no children of her own, I suppose she doesn't have much else to do but look out her window." Emily averted her eyes. "Actually I happened to be up very late last night myself—um, reading, and things like that. I heard your car pull in out front. I—I've gotten to recognize the slamming of your car door."

Luke accepted her explanation without comment and countered with one of his own, not that she had asked. "I was doing an initial reconstruct on a cleft palate yesterday," he told her, unwrapping the steaks and laying them, one by one, on the fire. "It wasn't a particularly involved surgery, but the child had some unexpected complications in the recovery room. A collapsed lung. You never know when something like that is going to happen. The anesthesiologist and I stayed at the hospital until the baby was out of danger."

He watched as her eyes clouded with sympathy. "Poor little thing. Is he all right now?"

The steaks had begun to sizzle and Luke waved his hand through the thick smoke that rose from the top of the grill. "*She*. And, yes, she's fine, Emily. The parents are still a little shaky, but she's fine. Hey," he said quickly when she continued to frown, "the child's all right, Emily. Honest."

She sighed, averting her head. "I know, Luke. I'm sure you're an excellent surgeon. It's just—well, it's just that if Michael or Sarah were ever to have a real medical crisis and I had to deal with it alone, I don't know if I could cope. It's one of the many things I think about sometimes, late at night when I—"

She stopped speaking and turned back to him, her smile bright. Too bright. As were her eyes. As if she was close to tears. "But I'd manage, Luke. I know I would. It just wouldn't be easy."

"Hardly anything ever is, Emily," Luke answered, his heart moved. "There's nothing more unnerving than the feeling of being helpless in the middle of a medical emergency. When my parents were injured, before they died, I felt completely useless and at my wits' end—and I'm a doctor. I watch the parents of my patients and sympathize with them, feel for them, do my best to calm their fears. But, outside of doing my best in the operating room, there's really little else I can do to help."

"I'm sure you have a very convincing bedside manner, Doctor," Emily told him, visibly relaxing. "However, I think you'd better turn over those steaks. They're beginning to burn."

Later, once they had all eaten—Luke gleefully accepting compliments on his cooking, and Emily busily replacing the cold salads in the cooler—Michael came up to Luke, his expression solemn, and asked if he could please talk with him. "Somewhere private," he said, exaggeratedly moving his eyes in the direction of his mother.

"Sure thing, kiddo," Luke answered, suddenly wary, but interested. He took the child's hand and walked toward the water, where Fred was turned onto his back on the grassy bank and sound asleep, completely ignorant of the basic rules of modesty. "What's up?"

Michael sat on the ground and began rubbing Fred's stomach, much to the delight of the dog, who stuck out his tongue and issued a great doggie sigh. "It's Mommy," the boy said, his big brown eyes troubled. "Do you think you could cut her open, Dr. Manning?"

Luke had been prepared to hear almost anything. Or so he thought. But Michael's bluntly worded request floored him. "Cut her open?" he repeated, trying to understand. "Why, Michael? Do you think Emily—I mean, do you think your mother is sick?"

Michael nodded. "I think she is, Dr. Manning. She's tired a lot, because she works so much, and she cries sometimes, like when I asked her who I could take to the father-and-son baseball banquet at the end of the season. That's in September, you know. Jason Hendricks is taking his dad, and Sheila Waters is taking her Uncle Jack, but I don't have anybody. And I think I'm going to get an award. Most improved player."

"I see," Luke said. And he did see. All too much; much more than Michael's words had told him, remembering that one of the children had said Emily sometimes cried at night. He felt out of his depth. *Way* out of his depth. "But what does any of this have to do with having me operate on your mother?"

Michael rolled his eyes, as if to say that he thought Luke to be unbelievably dense. "You're a repairman. You said that when you cut kids open you fix them, so that they can be happy again and go out and play like the other kids. Don't you remember?"

Oh, boy, did Luke ever remember! Emily said he must have a good bedside manner. Maybe. But he had a lousy way of expressing himself. "I remember, Michael, although this is a little different. Somehow I think you already know that. Your mommy isn't really physically sick, is she? Now why don't you tell me exactly what you want me to do?"

Michael pulled a face, as if what he was about to say was incredibly difficult. "Well, I guess I just want you to make my mommy happy again. I was in the dining room last night when Aunt Madge was in the kitchen having coffee with Mommy. I didn't mean to hear, or anything. I just did."

"Of course, Michael. And exactly what did you hear?"

"Aunt Madge said it wasn't right. She said that I should have a father to take me to the banquet, and that Sarah wouldn't cry so much if Mommy was home all day with her. And then Mommy started to cry, real soft, so that I could hardly hear her, and then Aunt Madge said—"

Luke silenced the boy with a quick wave of his hand. All of a sudden Emily's mood of an hour ago made perfect sense to Luke. No wonder she had been unable to sleep last night. "Never mind, Michael, I think I'm getting the general idea."

"Then you'll do it? You'll fix her?" Michael asked, his face suddenly wreathed in smiles. "Thanks, Dr. Manning. Aunt Madge said you were just the one Mommy needed!" he exclaimed, firmly patting Fred on the stomach. The dog turned over and stood up before running after the now rapidly retreating boy, who was heading in the direction of his sister, waving his arms excitedly as if he had wonderful news for her.

"Oh, brother," Luke said, resting his suddenly weary head in his hands. "Please allow me to offer you my congratulations, Dr. Manning," he muttered in consternation. "Thanks to a single friendly invitation to a dinner dance, a few casual outings—and some neighborly interference by one Madge Sinclair—I think you have just been nominated as Michael's new 'father.'"

So why was he still sitting here, acting as if Madge Sinclair might just be right? Why wasn't he running for the hills as fast as his legs could carry him?

He rolled onto his stomach, watching as Emily joined her children on the grass for a friendly game of badminton, and proceeded to give both those questions considerable thought.

Emily watched as Luke unbuckled Sarah from the seat belt and lifted her sleeping form into his arms. Then she hastened ahead of him to unlock the front door to her town house, with Michael and Fred bringing up the rear.

It had been a long but pleasant afternoon, and since Sarah was used to taking a nap Emily hadn't been surprised to see that the child had fallen asleep on the way home. What did surprise her was the way Luke had joined so completely in their fun, playing badminton, helping to launch a kite, and even teaching Michael how to bunt.

Every day Emily was seeing more facets of the man who had come into her life a little less than a month ago. And every day she was liking him better. Much better. *Handsome* was one thing. *Nice* was better.

If only Madge weren't so outspoken, putting ideas into Emily's head that had no real business being there. Yes, Luke was wonderful with the children. Yes, he was an extremely nice, extremely handsome and successful man; Madge always managed to remind her of Luke's profession.

Not that Luke's profession had anything to do with the way she was beginning to feel about him, unless she considered the fact that he was a very caring, giving man.

What she really liked was his sense of humor, and the way he was with Michael and Sarah, and his willingness to go slow where the two of them were concerned.

And the way he looked in a tuxedo, and the effect he had on her insides when he smiled at her, and the strange way she had of seeing him each time she closed her eyes at night.

She may as well face it. She, Emily Cornell, level-headed widow and mother of two, was definitely beginning to have something more than "friendly" feelings for one Doctor Luke Manning.

"Put her here," she said now, turning back the bed covers so that Luke could lay Sarah on the bed. "She'll probably wake in another hour or so, demanding to know how she got home. Then I can wash her face and hands and have her brush her teeth."

Luke bent over the bed, pressing a kiss on Sarah's forehead, shocking Emily into realizing she was suddenly jealous of her own daughter. She had better get control of herself and quickly. Luke had been very upfront with her, telling her he wanted to be friends. If she wanted more than that, and it certainly appeared as if she did, maybe it would be best if they called this off now. A person could get hurt otherwise. A person like herself, for instance.

"I asked Michael to put Fred inside the fence and then go over to Madge's for a few minutes, Emily," he said as they left the room, closing the door behind them. "Do you think we could go into the kitchen and talk for a minute?"

He seemed so serious. Surely he wasn't about to tell her that he was tired of being included in all their plans? Michael had asked Luke to the picnic, and he had seemed to enjoy himself. But how much time did an eligible man like Doctor Luke Manning want to spend playing "happy family" with a widow and her two young children?

Was that it? Was Luke about to beat her to the punch? It didn't seem fair. She hadn't even decided, really decided, to break off their relationship. Not yet. She wasn't ready yet to let him go. Couldn't they be friends just a little bit longer? Please?

"Talk?" Emily swallowed hard, leading the way down the steps. "Sure, Luke. Why not? Do you want some iced tea first?"

"All right," he said, pulling out what she had begun to think of as "Luke's chair," and sat down at the table. "I can unload the car later and put anything cold in my refrigerator until tomorrow."

Emily took two tall glasses from the cabinet and filled them with ice before pouring the tea from the container she kept in the refrigerator. "I have to thank you again for teaching Michael how to bunt," she said, putting the glasses on the table and sitting down, before her apprehension made her fall down. "I'm pretty good with some things, but I'm afraid I'm not up on all the fine points of the game."

That was it. She'd keep talking. Keep them both talking. Then maybe she wouldn't have to listen to what he really wanted to say.

"You're welcome," Luke said, before taking a long, cooling drink of his tea. "This is really good, Emily. You don't use a mix, do you?"

She shook her head, suddenly eager to explain. "I make sun tea—that is, I put tea bags in a glass container filled with water and set the whole thing out in the sun to brew while I'm at work. I read about the method in a magazine. It is good. And easy."

Luke sat back and scratched at the side of his head. "Good girl. First the baseball, and now the home-brewed tea. That's two perfect lead-ins you've given me, Emily," he said, smiling, "and you didn't even know it."

She cocked her head to one side, wishing for about the fiftieth time that day that she hadn't put her hair in a ponytail. She felt so unsophisticated, so gauche. She was sure none of the nurses at the hospital wore their hair in ponytails. Besides, how would they get them to fit under their caps—or maybe they don't wear caps anymore? *Emily!* she warned herself—*stop it!* "I'm sorry, Luke. I don't understand."

He leaned back in the chair, tipping it so that it rested only on its hind legs. "Of course you don't. I think I'd be worried if you did. But you're nothing like Madge Sinclair, thank goodness." He sat forward, so that the front legs of the chair crashed against the tile floor. "Tell me, Emily, have you ever considered getting married again?"

She was glad she had yet to take a sip of her iced tea, for if she had, surely Luke would now be behind her, slapping her on the back to keep her from choking. His question had been about as expected as the idea of her ever being announced as the big winner in the Pennsylvania Lottery. *"What?"* she croaked, barely able to speak. "I said I don't know much about baseball, Luke, but that question, as they say in the game, came straight out of left field."

"I know. For me, too." Luke reached across the table to take her hands in his. "But hear me out, Emily, okay?"

Something in his tone told her that he wasn't about to declare his undying love for her and then propose marriage. But then again, it didn't sound like he was about to say goodbye, either. What harm could it do to listen? "All right," she answered, unwilling to pull her hands free.

"Michael and Sarah need a father, Emily," he said, as if he were telling her something she didn't already know. "And I really think you could use a husband. It isn't easy owning a house and raising two children in today's world, not without some help."

Now he had told her two things she already knew. She didn't understand. What was he going to do next—draw her a diagram, maybe use props?

Suddenly, without warning, she felt angry. "Everybody's got advice. First Madge, and now you." Yep, Emily knew she was definitely angry, and growing more angry by the second. "Well, I'm listening. What do you suggest, Luke? Maybe I could put an ad in the paper? 'Needed: one father. Must be good with young children, know how to change leaking sink washers and fix stuck kitchen drawers. Keep Sunday nights free in order to put out the garbage. References required.'"

She pulled her hands from Luke's and stood up, nearly toppling the chair in her haste. Walking to the sink, she stood looking out over the backyard, her arms wrapped tightly about her waist. "My God, Luke—do you really think it's that simple? Besides, what makes you think I'd even want to marry again? I don't, you know. I don't even think about it." She had to look out over the backyard. She certainly couldn't look him straight in the eye and lie this way!

Oh, God. Luke was behind her. She didn't know how he had gotten there so quickly, but there he was, not inches from her, his voice low, rumbling and somewhat humble—each word tearing at her vulnerable heart. "Emily, I'm sorry. I didn't mean to insult your intelligence. This is kind of a spur-of-the-moment thing, and I haven't really had time to prepare a speech. Please, hear me out."

She bit down hard on the soft flesh of the inside of her cheek and nodded, unable to speak.

"I told you I was once engaged to be married," he said, his words gaining her full attention. "When Julia and I broke up I promised myself I wouldn't fall in love again. It hurt, losing Julia, and I don't like being hurt. But I love children, Emily. I love the idea of having a family."

He fell silent, so that she knew he was finding it difficult to continue. He certainly had captured her attention. And maybe her hopes. All right. She had been wrong. He wouldn't have to draw her a map. She knew—somehow she didn't quite know how, but somehow she knew—what he wanted to say.

Turning to face him, she offered helpfully, "I have two children, Luke. One ready-made family, living only five or six doors down the street from you. No muss, no fuss, no need for a courtship. Just four people all looking for the same thing. What could be more logical than for them to merge, become an instant family, with benefits on all sides? That *is* what you're getting at, isn't it?"

He turned away, a hand to his forehead. "Lord, it all sounds so cold the way you say it, so clinical. But, yes, that is what I'm getting at. And I'm not just thinking of myself. You and the kids would benefit as well, Emily. You could quit your job, be home all day with Sarah, and—well, Michael could have me as his guest at the father-and-son baseball banquet."

His last statement shook her more than anything that had come before it, and Emily felt her bottom lip begin to quiver. It had been stupid to cry over the fact that Michael had no one to take him to the father-and-son banquet. Stupid, and futile. "Michael told you about the banquet?"

"He told me."

"What else did he tell you?" Emily was beginning to have a very bad feeling about the conversation she'd had with Madge Sinclair yesterday. She had thought Michael was watching television in the living room, but obviously he had found time to listen to what Madge was saying in the kitchen—then run straight to Luke to repeat everything he'd heard. "Did he also tell you that I cried yesterday?"

Luke put his hands on her shoulders, so that Emily was sure she would have no choice but to start crying again, sobbing all over his navy golf shirt. "Forget all that, Emily. It doesn't really matter what Michael told me. I probably would have come to this same conclusion eventually myself. Michael's talk with me this afternoon only made me realize it sooner. Emily, our marriage could work."

"Because you love my children?" Emily knew her voice was not without sarcasm.

"And because I like you. And because I think you like me. I understand that you haven't really thought about marrying again. We've already had passion, Emily. You with your husband, and me with Julia.

What you and I have is a pleasant friendship—a great friendship, actually—with the children to give us even more in common. Then, in the future, if the two of us want it—maybe then we could have a real marriage. But for now, isn't half a loaf better than none?''

"If both of us want it," Emily repeated, her head reeling. So much for any thoughts of romance. There had been no romance in Mark's proposal, either. He had just begun talking about marriage while they were juniors in high school, as if she had already agreed.

But, oh, how she wanted some of the romance!

"We could have a real marriage if we both wanted it. That's an interesting statement. Tell me, Luke, how do we let each other know—send up flares?" She had been foolish to listen. This wouldn't work. It couldn't work. She was too aware of Luke the man. Not Luke the friend. She pulled away from him and walked into the living room. "Oh, Luke, I don't know—"

"And I don't blame you," he said, following her. "I should have gone home and thought this through, but the idea only occurred to me this afternoon—well, it just seemed like such a good idea that..." his words trailed off as he shrugged his shoulders.

Emily smiled. His expression reminded her of the way Michael had looked the day he had brought home the frog. He, too, had considered it to be a good idea at the time.

"I think—I think that it probably might be a good idea, Luke," she said hesitantly. "I mean, you are right that we get along. And the children do like you. Especially Michael. And they like Fred. And it would give me the chance to stay home with Sarah, if you're serious about my not having to work. As a matter of fact, all the positives seem to be adding up in my column. But what would you get from this marriage?''

His smile was slow, but it spread, reaching all the way up to his dark, penetrating eyes. "I already told you, Emily. I'd have a family.''

A family.

Emily's heart broke. Right there, in the middle of her living room, her heart broke.

She walked to the front door, opening it for him, praying he'd leave before she gave in, before she agreed to the insanity of a platonic marriage to a man whose smile turned her insides to jelly. Quickly, quickly. She had to get him out of her house. "Oh, of course. You'd have a family. Fred would like that. Can I have some time to think about it, Luke? At the risk of sounding coy... this is all quite sudden, you know. Oh, one thing more before you go, Luke. Would you want to put all of this in writing, some sort of prenuptial agreement? If I were to agree to the marriage, I mean.''

He shook his head. "A prenuptial agreement? No, I don't think so. As long as both of us understand the ground rules, I see no need to involve a lawyer, do you?''

Emily cringed inwardly at the thought of sitting in some paneled office, coldly writing down the words "platonic marriage." "No. No, I don't think we'd need to put the agreement in writing. I know I wouldn't have any trouble remembering the rules. I think they'd be pretty hard to forget, don't you?''

He leaned down and kissed her cheek, a gesture so blatantly *friendly* that she suddenly longed to hit him—or grab on to both his shoulders and pull him against her, showing him that she might be somebody's mother, but she did know how to kiss. She was longing to show him that she wanted to be kissed, needed to be kissed like any other woman. Perhaps more.

"I'll call you tomorrow? Michael has a game tomorrow night, doesn't he? We could go out afterward, for ice cream."

"That sounds lovely, Luke," she responded woodenly, stepping away from him, away from temptation. "You can pick us up at six, all right?"

A moment later he was gone, just as Michael came running down the pavement on his way back from Madge's and Sarah woke upstairs, calling for her mother.

Emily deliberately turned her back on thoughts of Luke's clinical proposal, thoughts of love and "happily ever after," and went about the mundane business of getting her children ready for bed.

She couldn't let the children see her cry.

Chapter Five

SCORPIO: You've been worrying if you've done the right thing. Plans recently begun progress, much to your delight. But are you really happy? Unforeseen circumstances cloud picture. Be patient; tamp down your sensual side. Clear heads must dominate.

Luke closed the door to his house and picked up the mail that had been pushed through the slot, sorting it as he walked to the kitchen in order to let Fred in from the backyard.

His hand stilled on the knob as he recognized Julia's flowing handwriting on a thick brown envelope marked "Photo—Do Not Bend." Fred forgotten, he sat at the table, holding the envelope in front of him, sure he already knew what he would find inside—a photograph of Julia and Max's son, Sean. The boy was about four months old now, just about the time proud parents began taking their children to photo studios and then sending out pictures of their beautiful child to everyone they knew.

He must have a dozen pictures of his friends' babies stuffed in a drawer in the dining room. Maybe two dozen. And he had stood as godfather to a half dozen more. All day at the hospital, he saw nothing but babies and young children.

He turned the envelope over, pushing a fingertip against the easy-open tab. Lots of children. Hundreds of children. All shapes. All sizes. All sexes. All colors.

There was only one really important difference about young Sean Rafferty. If things had worked out differently two years earlier, if there had been no Max Rafferty, this child might have been his.

Leaving the envelope on the table, Luke went in search of a cold can of soda before opening the door to Fred, who immediately launched his huge body into the kitchen, sliding to a halt halfway across the slippery tile floor.

He fed Fred, deliberately delaying the moment he would have to open the envelope and see Julia's son for the first time.

Fred had been Luke's answer to his loneliness two years ago, a companion in his solitude, his misery, the puppy helping to fill the void left by Julia's absence.

Everything Luke had done in the past two years had been in an effort to fill that void. Fred. His surgical practice. The long hours he put in at the hospital and at the free clinic. Long after he had stopped loving

Julia, wanting Julia, and had begun liking her, he had been struggling to find something to fill the yawning void in his life—searching for happiness. As a matter of fact, until Emily Cornell and her children had come into his life, he had been living each day in an effort to forget how close he had come to happiness, only to lose it.

Not that he was bitter, because he wasn't. He was incapable of such a feeling. He was genuinely happy for Julia and knew that breaking their engagement had been the only correct thing to do.

But the experience had hurt. It had hurt badly. And Luke knew he wasn't in the market to be hurt again. He had built a wall around his heart in order to protect himself from being hurt again, but he couldn't seem to banish the wish to belong to somebody, to have someone besides Fred to come home to at night. That's why his proposal to Emily, four days after he had presented his idea to her, still seemed to be a workable solution to his longing for a wife, a family of his own.

When he knew he had put it off long enough, when he knew it was stupid to put it off any longer, he sat at the table again and ripped open the envelope, spilling the picture onto the surface.

And then he laughed. He laughed until he had rid himself of any lingering pain, any last subconscious regrets for what might have been. The last bonds had been broken, leaving him free to begin looking for his own future.

Sean Rafferty was a carbon copy of his father, Max, right down to the most charming, self-possessed smile he'd ever seen on an infant. He could have picked the child out of a crowd of babies.

For the first time in more than two years, Luke felt whole again.

"Knock, knock."

Luke turned to see that Emily was standing outside the screen door leading to the backyard, a covered dish in her hands. Stuffing the picture back in the envelope, he placed it on the top of the refrigerator before opening the door. "Knock, knock, yourself. Something smells good."

Something looked good, as well: Emily. She had the most genuine smile he'd ever seen, honest and unaffected, if perhaps slightly shy. He watched as she placed the dish on the table, wondering what she would do if he leaned down and placed a kiss on her nape.

"I made a Crockpot meal this morning before I left for work and thought you might like some. I think I made enough for a small army. Michael's bringing up the rear with a tossed salad in hand, but Sarah has defected for the evening. She went to the mall with Madge to help her look for curtains for her spare bedroom. I have a hunch she was bribed with the promise of frozen yogurt once they're done shopping."

The whole time Emily had been talking she was preparing a place for him at his own table, already familiar with where he kept his dishes and utensils, her movements effortless and efficient. Luke stood back and let her have at it, the aroma of what had to be beef stew affecting him more than Nurse Watkins's perfume had as he'd gone over medical notes with her at the nurses' station that afternoon.

Yes, the idea of kissing Emily was growing more interesting by the moment. Lord, how he admired her red lipstick. Would her mouth taste like cherries?

"There you go, Luke," she said, lifting the lid of the bowl she had brought with her and signaling for him to sit, oblivious to his designs on her. "I hope you like it."

He did. Emily, he had learned, was an excellent cook. But it wasn't her cooking that made the meal pleasant.

It was having her sit across the table from him while he ate stew and salad, talking about the events of the day with him while Michael and Fred played together in the backyard.

Piercing the center of a small cherry tomato, he held out the fork in Emily's direction. "Here. You've been staring at it long enough. Take a bite."

"Oh, you noticed that, did you? I really shouldn't. I had plenty with my own dinner—oh, all right." She leaned forward across the table and he fed her the ripe, red tomato, smiling as he watched her lips close around it, still smiling as she closed her eyes in ecstasy as she chewed.

Although he was nearly through with his meal, Luke realized that he was suddenly ravenous. But his hunger had nothing to do with a need for food. He was hungry to know the taste of Emily's mouth. His arms were ravenous to hold her. His appetite for the stew faded, to be replaced with a growing appetite for Emily Cornell.

He speared another tomato and again offered it to Emily before taking a last bite of beef stew, feeling as if they were recreating, in a much more refined, tasteful way, the eating scene in the movie *Tom Jones*.

Shaken by this rush of passion for the woman to whom he had proposed a platonic marriage, Luke hastily picked up his plate and took it to the sink, ordering himself to stop thinking like a man who was looking for romance—because he wasn't, damn it. If he didn't watch himself, rein in his traitorous thoughts, he'd scare her away.

"Here," Emily said, coming up beside him, the salad plate and his utensils in hand. "I cooked. You wash up. I call that a fair division of labor, don't you?"

He didn't look at her. He couldn't look at her. If he did, if he turned so much as an inch in her direction, he would have to kiss her. And if he kissed her, if he showed her even a small inkling of the sudden, fierce passion he felt for her, she would most probably run screaming out of the house.

"Emily," he said, clearing his throat, pushing down the urge to call her "darling," or "sweetheart." "Have you given any more thought to my proposal?"

She placed the dish and utensils in the sink and returned to sit at the table, picking up his paper napkin and folding it neatly in half before crushing it into a ball. "Luke—it's only been four days. I—I haven't had much time to think about it. But, yes, I have been considering what you said. I think—"

"Dr. Manning?"

Michael opened the screen door, and he and Fred tumbled into the kitchen, both of them looking happily disheveled. "I think Fred wants a drink of water. I know I do. Is there any juice, please? You had orange juice yesterday when Sarah and I were here."

Luke looked toward Emily, who was now concentrating on shredding the napkin into a thousand small pieces, and he wished Michael had gone to the mall with his sister. But he hadn't.

"Sure, tiger," he said. "There's still some left in the refrigerator. You get it while I find us some glasses. Emily?"

"Thank you, no," she answered, rising as she shoved the remains of the napkin into her skirt pocket. "I'll leave you two gentlemen to your drinks. I have to go home now. I have laundry to do. Um—Luke? Do you think you could come over later, perhaps after the children are in bed?"

He only had time to nod his agreement before Emily told Michael to be a good boy and departed, leaving Luke to look after her thoughtfully, wondering what she would have told him if her son hadn't interrupted them—and worrying that he might not want to hear what she said.

Emily paced the width of her bedroom, mentally kicking herself for spending the last four days conjuring up images of her and Luke as a happily married couple.

Luke wasn't interested in their being a couple—he wanted a family. He had been more than explicit on that point. He had been brutally honest. The only reason she had even been included in his proposal was because he couldn't figure out a way to get Michael and Sarah without taking her along, as well. They were a package deal.

Of course, she would come in handy whenever he needed a female on his arm, like for board of directors' dinner dances. And she did cook a tolerable meal.

But as for passion, as for love—well, Luke Manning obviously wasn't interested. How else could she explain his cool detachment earlier, when he had fed her the tomatoes? She had thought he had been flirting with her, had believed he, like she, could feel an attraction growing between them, an attraction that had nothing to do with anything so clinically detached as a marriage of convenience.

She had been wrong.

"Boy, was I wrong!" she said now, picking up her brush and pulling it through her shoulder-length hair, catching at a knot so that tears stung her eyes. "Yet I was the one who told him I wasn't looking for love again. I'm the one who informed him I hadn't planned to marry again. Why did I lie to him? Why have I been lying to myself? What am I afraid of? Hasn't Mark been dead long enough for me to have put the past behind me?"

She ran a hand through her hair, then glared into the mirror once more. "Besides, Luke is the one that seems to think I would be amenable to a platonic marriage. How did he get that impression? Where does it say that widows don't want—or need—romance? Where is it written that a woman, on becoming a mother, no longer requires courting, sweet words or toe-curling kisses? I'm twenty-six, not a hundred and twenty-six. Why do I bring out the nesting instinct in this man, but not his passions?"

She stopped brushing her hair and leaned forward, looking into the mirror above her dresser, studying her reflection as if for an answer to her questions, then groaned.

Her very ordinary light brown hair was cut in a nononsense style, neat, easily kept, but far from sophisticated. Her makeup consisted of blush, mascara and a hint of red lipstick. She didn't even *own* foundation or an eyelash curler.

As for her clothes, well, she certainly couldn't compete with Julia Sutherland Rafferty's designs. The Sutherland line was carried where she worked, so she should know. But cotton was serviceable, easily laundered, and there wasn't much room for high-fashion, high-priced clothes in a budget that also paid for babysitting and dentist bills.

"Emily," she said, grimacing at her reflection, "face it. You *look* like somebody's mother. You look like someone who goes to Parent and Teacher Night, someone who helps make native huts out of painted Popsicle sticks, someone who spends her Saturday nights clipping cents-off coupons for the supermarket. You do not, in short, look like anyone's vision of a woman ripe for romance. You're brownies and cold milk, not caviar and champagne."

She continued to look into the mirror, wondering why, at the age of twenty-six, she was considering a marriage rich in everything but love. Because she *was* considering it.

And then she smiled. Luke *had* fed her the tomato. He *had* kissed her on the cheek. And he *had* held her fairly close when they had danced. She might be twenty-six, but he wasn't more than thirty-five. Neither one of them was exactly ready for the rocking chair.

He liked her. He wanted to marry her. If Madge Sinclair had two children like Michael and Sarah she doubted if Luke would have proposed to her! Maybe it was up to her, to Emily Cornell, *woman,* to show Dr. Luke Manning that there could be more to this marriage than he had first supposed.

And *that's* why she was considering Luke's offer— and their unwritten prenuptial agreement. Because she could love him. He could love her.

Someday.

She was still smiling a half hour later when the doorbell rang, announcing Luke's arrival. Her hair freshly combed, her light red lipstick and her smile in place, Emily rose from the couch and answered the door.

"Hello again, Luke," she said, taking the now-clean dish from him as he stepped inside the small foyer. He had changed into a white knit shirt and casual tan slacks since she had last seen him, banishing any trace of the important pediatric surgeon and leaving behind the handsome man who seemed to enjoy spending his evenings in the bleachers watching a gang of six-year-olds battle to a ludicrous thirty-nine to twenty-six victory on the baseball diamond.

He sat on the couch as she poured them each a glass of lemonade from the pitcher she had prepared only a few minutes earlier. "So, Emily," he asked as she joined him, "are the kids asleep now? Fred is stretched out in my living room, snoring. I think Michael must have worn him out."

She nodded, carefully replacing her glass in the coaster, tinglingly aware of the fact that he was no more than six inches away. She looked at his hands, the long, well-sculptured hands that held a scalpel, and a child's life, in his care every day. She had only to move, to reach out, and she could touch those hands.

Emily averted her eyes and her thoughts, both of which were beginning to prove treacherous. "Yes, they're sleeping. Um, Luke—I asked you over tonight so that we could talk without interruption. About that proposal—I mean, that proposition you made."

"You had it right the first time, Emily. It's not a proposition. It's a proposal," he corrected her, smiling, so that she was struck yet again by how straight and even his white teeth were and how good he looked with his skin tanned. He hadn't been nearly so tan when they'd first met. If nothing else, she and the children had gotten him out into the sunlight. "I've been thinking about that, too, which is something I probably should have done before springing it on you the way I did. I was only looking at how much I stood to gain from this marriage. I really wasn't being fair to you four days ago, Emily."

Fair? What did any of this have to do with being fair? And why did they both sound so formal, so stilted? Suddenly, as she looked into Luke's eyes, as she glimpsed the vulnerability he went to such great lengths to hide, saw and recognized the pain and the loneliness, she panicked at the thought that this wonderful man might be about to say something that would take him out of her life.

He was going to be a gentleman and withdraw his proposal. He was going to give her an out, a reason to make her excuses and call a halt to what he had begun.

Oh, no, he wasn't!

"I've decided to marry you!" she blurted out quickly, forestalling him.

"Really? Emily, that's terrific!"

She grinned. "Yeah. Yeah, it is, isn't it?"

Before she could think of anything else to add, Luke leaned over and kissed her on the cheek. "Then it's settled. Since neither of us has any close family, we can be married quietly. August would be good. Before the father-and-son banquet."

"August? I guess that would be good." How could she be speaking so calmly? What had she done? Emily's head began to spin and she only nodded again, afraid to say more, afraid that if she did open her mouth even one more time tonight she would blurt out something stupid, like, "You're sealing our engagement by kissing me on the cheek? Isn't that taking this friendship business a little too literally? Don't you find me even *slightly* attractive?"

He frowned. "Does it bother you that I would be going to the banquet in Mark's place?"

"What?" Emily stiffened at the mention of her late husband's name. This may not be the most romantic of proposals, but did Luke have to dash cold water on her by mentioning Mark's name? "I really don't want to talk about Mark with you, Luke, if that's all right. Just," she added, feeling a small spark of rebellion, "as I don't think I need to hear the name Julia again in the near future. Not if we're going to be married. Ours may be a marriage based on friendship, but I'm not that much of a good sport."

Married! She still couldn't believe it. She was actually sitting in the middle of her living room—with a basket of folded laundry staring at her from across the room—discussing marriage in the same sort of tone she would use in picking out a new carpet. Without a word of love, without even so much as a single *real* kiss, a single caress. No stars in her eyes or the sound of bells ringing in her ears. No romance at all. And yet she had said yes.

It was ludicrous!

But it was happening.

"Agreed," Luke said, looking very much like a man who had accomplished what he had set out to do and now wanted to be somewhere else. Anywhere else. "We'll tell the kids together, if you want. Tomorrow night?"

Emily mumbled her agreement, then followed Luke to the door, suddenly wanting him gone as much as, if not more than, he seemed to wish for the same thing. She stood there watching him go down the street, one hand pressed against her cheek where his lips had touched it.

The phone rang, but she ignored it, knowing it would be Madge, who must have set up camp at her front window, waiting for Luke to leave. She couldn't talk to Madge now, couldn't field questions from the well-meaning but nosy neighbor. She needed a few minutes alone to absorb everything that had just happened. Maybe a month wouldn't be long enough.

She was engaged to be married. She, Emily Cornell, had just become engaged to marry Dr. Luke Manning. *Unbelievable!*

Her children would have a father, her financial worries would be over, and maybe—someday—she would actually have a husband in every sense of the word. That was the "dream" part of her scenario, the part that gave a rosy color to the rest of it.

And why not? Luke had said they were friends, but that didn't mean that they couldn't one day be lovers.

Stranger things had happened. After all, what could be stranger than his proposal and her acceptance?

She should be happy. Deliriously happy.

The phone began to ring again and she raised her fingers to her cheeks, realizing that they were wet.

She should be happy. So how come she was crying?

Chapter Six

JULY 17:
YOUR DAILY ASTROLOGICAL FORECAST

SCORPIO: Your stars today point to new starts, new directions. Possible change in domicile, living arrangements. Children, pets involved. Avoid confrontations, be willing to negotiate in hopes of building on a firmer base.

"But this is only six or seven blocks from where we already live!" Emily exclaimed as they drove into the new development of single-family homes situated just behind Cedar Crest Boulevard and no more than three miles from the hospital where Luke practiced.

"I'm surprised, too," Luke said, parking in front of one of the three sample homes. "Ben Easterly told me about this place—said it was really shaping up into a fine area—but I hesitated to come here because we're looking for a completed house. But after the horrors we've already toured this weekend, I thought we might as well come see what all the shouting's about.''

Emily was confused. It would take six months before they could have a house built. Maybe a year. As Luke had just said, they had decided to buy a house—not build one.

Looking around, she saw station wagons in driveways, swing sets in backyards, and children riding their bicycles on the pavements. It was a lovely area! ''Several of them are already inhabited. I knew homes were being built here, Luke, but I had no idea it had gotten to this stage.''

The other houses they'd looked at had just been houses, masses of stone and wood and plaster that hadn't meant much to her. But these houses! Everywhere she looked there were signs of people who were investing time and money into making their houses into homes. Real homes. Real permanence. Real commitment.

A person living in one of these houses might begin to believe she was really married. Might even start thinking about having more children who could play in the yard, swing on the swings and ride their bikes up and down the broad sidewalks.

Emily remained in the car, her hand frozen on the handle of the opened door, unwilling to step onto the pavement—or afraid to. She really didn't think it was a good time to investigate her motives. It was much too soon to start pinning her hopes on the stars.

They had all piled into Luke's car three long hours ago, a low-slung sports car that Michael had thought was ''real neat'' until yesterday, when he had learned he had to sit in the back with his sister as they'd traveled from one Open House to another and discovered that, even at his size, there wasn't enough leg room for him.

Today, for the past three *long* hours they had been driving around the Allentown suburbs, attending even more Open Houses and jotting down addresses of likely looking houses with For Sale signs on the lawn— Luke intent on finding them a home before the weekend was out.

She had been learning a lot about Luke Manning since they had decided on their arrangement. Emily had decided to refer to it in her mind as just that, an "arrangement," for she had already found that to think of what they were doing as a marriage undermined her budding confidence that things would one day be different.

Luke was a "get it done yesterday" kind of man. He made up his mind and then went about whatever project it was with a single-minded devotion that had already begun to rub off on her. It was a complete reversal of Mark's attitude about life. It had taken him six months to decide what color he wanted to paint the living room. Spring green. She had hated that shade, not that Mark had asked her opinion.

Now that she thought of it, she hadn't made a single decision on her own, either before or during their entire marriage. When they would marry, where they would live, what they would name their children— everything had been Mark's decision. Including his decision to quit college in his junior year and join the fire department as his father had before him.

But she didn't have time now to think about Mark, about the profession that had taken both Mark and, a year later, his father, or even about spring green paint.

She'd had more than four long, difficult years in which to make decisions on her own. She had grown up, whether she'd wanted to or not, and it had been *her* decision to sell the house she and Mark had lived in with his father, *her* decision to move into one of the town houses in the suburbs of Allentown, *her* decision to make every *decision* on her own.

And, boy, oh, boy, her *latest* decision had been a real doozy! She was going to be married!

After setting a date for their wedding, a house seemed to be the next item on Luke's mental agenda, and it appeared that he wasn't going to rest until he found one.

All her arguments that they could move into either one of the town houses had fallen on deaf ears— Luke's and Michael's and Sarah's. No, both houses were to be sold, and the For Sale sign had gone up on Luke's town house yesterday. Tomorrow it would be her turn to sign with the Realtor. It was a big step, but Luke's arguments had convinced her a new house was best for everyone.

Fred and the children needed more room to roam, Luke had pointed out rationally, as well as teasing that however well-meaning Madge Sinclair could be, he didn't think he wished to continue living six doors down the street from the woman.

Michael had put up a bit of a fuss until Luke explained that he wouldn't be moving outside his current school district or away from his baseball team, at which point the boy had immediately begun packing his toys in anticipation of the move.

Sarah, bless her, hadn't voiced an opinion either way. All she knew was that her mommy was going to be home with her every day. For Sarah, who didn't seem to like having Emily out of sight, let alone out of the house, that appeared to be enough.

But the argument that had settled it for Emily, the one argument Luke had been gracious enough not to point out to her, was that both of their houses were alike. Both of them had only three bedrooms.

Emily had already handed in her notice at the boutique, thinking that she would stay on for another two weeks, but the owner, who had become less than tolerant of Emily since she had refused a promotion that would entail having to work nights and weekends, had declared Emily to be "disloyal" and demanded that she leave the same day.

Emily hadn't argued. She had enough to do at home; going through packing boxes she had yet to empty after the move last fall, sorting out all of their belongings so that she didn't move things to the new house only to end up discarding them, and giving the remainder of Mark's already-packed clothing to charity. Why she had saved any of his belongings, above some personal items for the children, she didn't know, but the time had come to dispose of them.

If only she could clean out the closets in her mind as easily, lay fresh mental shelf paper and begin anew, without any traces of leftover emotional baggage still stuffed into the corners.

"Emily? This is the last house this morning, I promise," Luke said, standing next to the open door she was still clinging to, lost in thought. "Then we'll break for lunch and begin again. Okay?"

She turned to gather up her purse, then joined Luke and the children on the pavement, looking up at the fully landscaped sample home. "It's certainly big, isn't it? But, Luke, it would take forever to have one of these built. What happens if our houses sell quickly? Besides, I can already tell that it would cost a fortune."

Luke smiled at her, then took her hand as they headed up the curving brick path to the front door, the children running ahead of them. "Emily, everything costs a fortune these days. Besides, what harm can there be in just looking?"

Emily barely heard him. All she was aware of was the touch of his hand on hers, the gentle heat that radiated from him to her—and the lump that had suddenly formed in her throat. Lord, had it been that long since someone had held her hand?

No, it was Luke's touch that had prompted this reaction. Only *his* touch.

And if he didn't stop smiling at her that way her kneecaps were going to dissolve.

"Pretty brick," she mumbled, looking up at the two-story house. "And I like those windows," she commented, regarding the dozen Romanesque-pane topped windows—especially the huge one just above the double front doors—that were spaced so precisely along the width of both levels. "I wonder how you're supposed to wash them."

"A big ladder and a very long hose?" Luke suggested, opening the front door and ushering her inside after the children. "Wow! Look at this!"

Wow was right, Emily echoed silently, craning her neck to look around the large, two-story foyer. She could easily fit her entire living and dining room area into this space and still have room left over for half her kitchen.

The stairs, directly across from the front door, were carpeted in a deep mossy rose and swept to a wide landing before turning to the left and rising again to a balcony ringed by a beautiful mahogany-topped white wooden railing.

The chandelier suspended from the cathedral ceiling was a mass of elegant crystal prisms. Its light, which was on even now, shone softly on off-white walls accented by varying sizes of rectangles fashioned of thin, white wood framing. Inside several of these spaces were beautifully framed paintings—or perhaps prints—depicting a variety of lovely country scenes.

To her left, Emily could see a large living room, complete with fireplace, and to her right was a glass-door entrance to a formal dining room. Both rooms and the foyer they stood in were completely furnished in lovely eighteenth-century mahogany pieces, and the walls, painted in neutral colors, were topped by lovely wallpaper borders.

The color schemes in all three rooms were of soft mauve, Wedgewood blue and white.

Her favorite colors. And without a hint of spring green to be seen.

"There are even silk flowers on the dining-room table—and china place settings." Emily turned to Luke, her voice dropping to a whisper. "Are you sure somebody doesn't live here?"

"Hello."

Emily nearly jumped out of her skin as she turned to see a sleek, well-dressed redhead, wearing a close-fitting blue sheath and a pained smile, approach from the hallway. The door she came from was beneath the second level of the stairs, and Emily supposed it led to the kitchen.

"My name is Monica Woodward. I'm your sales agent. Could the two children in the family room be yours? They're sitting on one of the couches." The woman's tone implied that if these were their children, she would like to see them and Emily and Luke removed from the premises as quickly as possible.

Emily was all for telling Michael and Sarah to behave themselves, mentally picturing the couches in the family room to be white—and probably velvet.

Obviously Luke, who continued to hold her hand, had other ideas. "Ms. Woodward," he said, his tone very professional and more than a little cold, "my name is Luke Manning, and this is Emily Cornell. The children's names are Sarah and Michael. We would prefer it if you stayed with the children while my fiancée and I tour the upstairs. Then, once we have completed our inspection, we'll join you in the family room to discuss the particulars."

Emily stifled the urge to applaud. She knew she could have put the woman firmly in her place if she had wanted to—after all, Michael and Sarah weren't *jumping* on the couches—yet—but it was nice not to have to do everything for herself. It was also nice to hear herself referred to as Luke's fiancée. Very nice.

Monica Woodward opened her mouth as if to refuse, then seemed to think better of it. "Of course, Mr. Manning," she said, as Luke smiled at her. That smile was devastating. Emily ought to know, for she had seen it before. That's how she had gotten into this mess in the first place. "I'd be delighted to be of service. Then, if you have any questions, I'll be happy to answer them for you. And remember, please, that this is only one floor plan. We have several models to choose from, all equally lovely."

Once the sales agent had disappeared down the hallway, Emily giggled. "So that's how you keep all those nurses in line, Dr. Manning. I wondered how you managed it."

"I hope Sarah asks to go to the bathroom. It would serve that woman right," Luke muttered, looking down the hallway. Then he shook his head, his smile once more solidly in place. "Come on, Emily, let's see the upstairs. I think I like this place."

"Now there's a surprise, Luke. Who wouldn't like it?"

By the time Emily had seen three of the bedrooms and the large family bathroom, she more than liked the house. She loved it.

"You know, of course," Emily pointed out as they were leaving the smallest bedroom, "that it won't look this good without all the custom wallpaper and beautiful furniture. That's a clever marketing tactic, meant to make you forget that the house you get will have bare walls and all the furniture you bought years ago and have learned to hate. We did it with the dresses at the shop where I worked. That size six a customer sees on the mannequin is supposed to make her believe it will look just as good on her size-fourteen figure.''

Luke, who'd been noticeably silent since Emily had stood in the middle of the second bedroom and commented that it could be used as hers, only nodded and put a hand on her shoulder while he guided her toward the end of the large hallway and the final door.

She sensed that he had been hurt by her comment. But why? What else was she to say? Their ''agreement'' had been very clear, put forth by him and accepted by them both—even if she did dream that things might one day be different. She sighed, wondering for about the hundredth time whether or not Luke's plan would work.

The room they entered was positioned above the two-car garage and had a cathedral ceiling as well as a small area toward the front of the house furnished as a sitting room. The king-size bed looked almost small in the large room, although Emily knew herself to be very much aware of it.

''Shall we look at the bathroom?'' Luke said, causing Emily to believe that the bedroom—and the bed— made him uncomfortable, as well.

Emily went first, stopping in the small hallway that led to the back of the house to admire the built-in sink and dressing table to her left. The walk-in closet on her right was, as she told Luke, larger than Sarah's bedroom.

But it was the bathroom that made her heart start to pound. It was the bathroom that made it impossible for Emily to continue to pretend only a polite interest in the house.

She stepped into the room and immediately felt as if she were outdoors, standing in a lovely, secluded rain forest. Most of the large room was glass, and what wasn't was mirrored, reflecting the natural light. There were plants all around the huge tub that was enclosed in a platform reached by climbing two tiled levels encircling the base. A large glass shower occupied one corner, and there were matching sinks on either side of the tub's platform.

Now *this,* she thought, was what the magazine articles meant when they said to find yourself a retreat and take a half hour out of your day to indulge yourself—and not in a narrow tub squeezed into a tiny bathroom, its rim stacked with children's toys!

She stood very still while Luke walked over to peek into the tub. "It's equipped with a whirlpool, Emily. As a matter of fact, if we could find a way to attach a motor and steering wheel, I think we could take this baby for a ride down the Little Lehigh River."

His joke was enough to relax her, soothing over the roughness of having to inspect beautifully furnished bedrooms with the man she was going to marry, live with, but not really live with.

"I doubt even Michael would refuse to take a bath if he could take it in that tub," Emily said as they retraced their steps and walked down the hallway that led, as Emily had supposed, into the kitchen.

"Oh, my!" As she had expected, the kitchen was huge and equipped with every built-in convenience known to man, including a large center island that sported an indoor grill with a large copper exhaust fan rising above it to the ceiling.

She forgot that Luke was present, forgot any pretext of only showing a mild interest in the house, deserting him in her rush to peer into cabinets, spin the corner lazy Susan, run her fingertips along the miles of countertop and inspect the deep pantry placed next to the refrigerator.

"Look at this," Luke said, claiming her attention, and Emily turned to see that he was standing in what had to be the family room, a large area to the left of the kitchen designed with two pairs of French doors that led out to what she could see was a large, wraparound wooden deck.

There was even a small bar tucked into an alcove at the far end of the enormous room. The couches, she registered randomly, were not white velvet, but a sturdy muted plaid of mauve and blue. The seats of the four chairs surrounding a game table were upholstered in matching materials.

"It's a wet bar," Luke told her as Emily descended the two carpeted steps into the family room and joined him. "This is a perfect room for entertaining guests. The builder thought of everything."

"Yes," Emily agreed, smiling weakly. "It does seem as if he's thought of everything. I wonder what *everything* costs."

"Mommy!"

Emily turned to see Michael and Sarah entering the kitchen from what she thought would be the laundry area and garage, their faces bright and smiling. "Where's Miss Woodward?"

"She's got another customer, Mommy," Sarah said. "She wanted to give each of us a quarter to go find you, but we told her we can't take money from people anymore. Isn't that right, Michael?"

"Mom, did you look over here?" Michael asked, pointing to a small hallway cut into the kitchen that Emily had yet to inspect, though she was sure it led directly into the dining room. "There's this whole wall of doors, and even a little sink with a funny-looking faucet. The lady said it was a butler's pantry. Are we going to have a butler?"

Luke and Emily duly inspected the butler's pantry, which was as Michael had described it, a ten-foot-long built-in mahogany cabinet placed between the kitchen and the dining room. "No, Michael," Emily explained. "We're not going to have a butler. That's only an expression. See these upper cabinets, the ones with the glass doors? That's where people keep their good crystal and china."

Michael frowned. "That's too bad. If we had a butler, he could fix my bike chain when it comes off."

Luke ruffled Michael's hair. "Butlers don't do that sort of stuff, kiddo. From now on, I'll be fixing your bike chain, okay?"

Michael smiled up at Luke, his small face beaming with pleasure. "You're gonna be my dad, right, Dr. Manning? Just like all my friends have dads." He turned to Emily. "Mom," he said, the term, and his demeanor suddenly much more grown-up than the "Mommy" he used to call her, "Aunt Madge was right. This is going to be great!"

Sudden tears stung Emily's eyes and she turned away, pretending an interest in what lay behind the door across from the butler's pantry. It was time to put her own dreams aside and concentrate on the fact that this marriage, no matter how they allocated the sleeping arrangements, was primarily going to benefit Michael and Sarah. She opened the door to see that the large closet had been fitted with built-in shelves and a sewing machine.

"That's our sewing-and-crafts center," Monica Woodward said, startling Emily, who hadn't heard her approach. "It could be used as almost anything, I suppose, and as it has no window it probably would work best as a closet, but the interior designer fitted it out as a sewing room. Not that *anyone* sews anymore."

"I do," Emily said in a small voice, disliking the sophisticated Ms. Woodward more with each passing moment. The woman didn't have the faintest idea what she was selling. This wasn't just any house, any piece of property.

This was a home. A home to raise children in, a home that was a haven from the outside world, a place to plant roots, live in and dream in and grow old in, watching her children and her garden mature; a place where the whole family would gather to celebrate Thanksgiving and Christmas, and her children's children would come to spend the night with their Grandma and Grandpa.

"Or at least I used to sew," Emily remarked a few moments later, smiling weakly at Luke as she turned away from the sight of the custom-designed shelves which could hold spools of thread and bobbins and lengths of material, "when I had the time. Come along, children." It was time, Emily decided, that Cinderella left the ball.

"You can exit through the garage and office area which lie beyond the utility room and half bath," Monica said, motioning for them to follow her as she swung into her sales pitch. "It's a two-car garage, naturally, with room for a workshop if desired. This being the sample, we've added two offices and another bath at the rear, but the standard home does not include this area. As for the fireplaces, the one in the living room is standard, but those you saw in the family room and master suite are optional. The carpeting and parquet flooring used in this sample is also an option, although the treatment that is included is very nice, if not as plush. The master bath isn't optional, but the window treatment and platform tub are both extras. Also, the kitchen cabinets have been upgraded in this model and the wet bar and outside deck, of course, are not included."

"What else is optional?"

Emily turned to stare at Luke. "I think the air is free," she quipped, feeling waspish. Hadn't the man been listening? Didn't he understand the game? How had he purchased his first house without learning that the model home is always the most expensive? First they made you fall in love with the place, and then they started taking it apart, piece by agonizing piece, until you were left with a shell of what you loved.

Rather, she thought, the way a person visualizes the perfect marriage, only to have it stripped down to the bare bones, showing all the flaws and imperfections you didn't see when your eyes were dazzled by your youth and the stars and the dream. Now why had she thought of that? She felt a sudden chill in the air-conditioned office.

She put a hand on his arm. "Luke—let's go. Remember, you promised us lunch."

The children were inspecting the piles of carpeting arranged along one wall of the garage, Sarah seeming to have grown tired of playing with the sample kitchen-cabinet doors hung on one of the walls, each slam of one of the doors causing Ms. Woodward to flinch.

The sales agent smiled at Luke and handed him her card. "Your fiancée appears to be weary, Mr. Manning. Perhaps you'd like to stop back later, without the children, and we can discuss the details then. We're open until six this evening."

"Dr. Manning," Luke corrected, taking the card. "And thank you. We'll do that. Come on kids, house hunting is over for the day. Hamburgers, fries and extra-thick milk shakes await."

Emily was still frowning when they got back in the car. "Surely we're not going back, Luke? I mean, what's the point? Besides the fact that we'd have to wait for a house to be built, by the time we added even a quarter of the options the house would cost a fortune. Yet to live in a cut-rate version of that house would be terrible. I'd much rather we forgot the whole thing."

"I liked it, and so did you," Luke said, steering the car away from the curb. "I even liked the furniture. My stuff is all modern. I bought it all in one night, not really caring what it looked like as long as it was comfortable. What's the correct term for the style of the furniture in the sample? It's more like some of yours."

Emily laughed. "It's a new twist on an old style, actually. I think it's called Early Expensive. And I agree. It's beautiful. Someday, when I'm rich and famous, I'm going to fill a house with furniture like that from attic to cellar. Mine is all bargain-basement reproductions."

"I thought you liked it. It reminded me of you."

"It did?" She turned in her seat to look at him owlishly. "Are you saying that I look expensive?"

He shook his head. "No. That's not what I meant. The furniture looked warm and sort of 'homey'—I don't know if that's the right word, but you know what I mean. You looked good in that house, Emily. Happy."

This had gone far enough! She held up her hands, shaking her head. "I agree that it's a lovely home, but it's totally out of the question, Luke."

"Why?"

This question came from Michael, who had unbuckled his seat belt and was now leaning over the front seat.

"Michael, sit back and buckle up!" Emily ordered, her head suddenly beginning to pound. Things were moving too fast for her and had been ever since she'd agreed to this marriage that wasn't really a marriage. Now Luke was holding out yet another impossible dream. Only this time she wasn't going to listen!

"Yes, Emily. Why?" Luke asked as they pulled into the fast-food restaurant the children had listed as their choice of where to eat lunch. "If it's the cost that's bothering you, please don't worry about it. I was my parents' only heir, I haven't exactly been living the high life, and I make a good living. A damn good living, actually. Combine that with the equity I have in the town house, and I don't see where there would be any problem."

She shook her head, waiting until the children were seated and she and Luke were standing in line to buy lunch. "It's just wrong, Luke," she whispered, very aware that they were in the middle of a crowded restaurant. "You've already refused to use any money from the sale of my house to pay for a new one, making me promise to put it all in the bank for Michael and Sarah's education. Now you're acting like you want to build an expensive new house. I'm getting all the benefits here, Luke. Me—and Michael and Sarah."

She looked around to be sure no one was close enough to overhear and added, "Luke, I—I don't know if I can go through with this."

"Sure you can." He leaned down, placing a kiss on her cheek. How she adored it when he kissed her on the cheek. If only she had the courage to turn her head so that he could reach her mouth. "And you're wrong, Emily. The house we'll live in is nothing, no matter which one we buy. It's just window dressing. If it turns out to be window dressing that appeals to us, that makes us happy, then that's wonderful. But don't ever try to compare a house with you and Michael and Sarah—with my new family. Believe me, Emily, I'm the one who's getting the best deal here. The way I see it, I'm the luckiest man in the world.''

He slid his arm around her waist and pulled her close, giving her what she was sure he meant as a friendly hug.

And that's when—right there, standing third in line at the fast-food restaurant—Emily Cornell knew that she was in big trouble. It hadn't been merely wishful thinking, or a dream of romance. This was real. This was forever.

She had gone beyond the dream and fallen completely, totally and quite irrevocably in love with her "friend" and fiancé, Luke Manning.

Luke stood in the master suite, gazing up at the two large skylights that brought natural light into the room, while Monica Woodward sat on the striped satin love seat, her fingers flying over the keys of her pocket calculator. For one blinding instant he imagined he could see Emily and himself lying on the bed, wrapped in each other's arms as they watched the stars floating above their heads. He blinked and the vision vanished. The vision, but not the dream.

There he went again, counting his chickens. He had to remember their agreement. He had to remember to go slow. But that didn't mean he couldn't give his bride-to-be a wedding present, did it?

"When you say 'completely furnished,' Ms. Woodward, exactly what do you mean?"

"Well, Doctor, as I said, since we're talking about you purchasing this model, which we would only allow because of the current downturn in the upper-scale housing market, 'furnished' means that we won't be stripping off any of the wallpaper or removing any of the installed options. The price I've quoted you includes everything you see, the fireplaces, the kitchen cabinets and grill, the extra rooms you say you plan to use as a home office—we are zoned for professional use such as physicians' offices—everything except the furniture and draperies."

Luke walked into the bathroom, smiling as he recalled the look on Emily's face when she had first seen the room, that smile broadening as he remembered how she had looked as she rushed around the kitchen, peeking into each and every cabinet. Imagine the brownies she could come up with in that kitchen!

This was Emily's house. He knew it. She knew it. It had been obvious to both of them the minute they had stepped into the foyer.

The purchase price was steep, but less than he had imagined, although he was sure Emily would have paled when Ms. Woodward hit the total button and announced the amount.

How many houses did a man buy in a lifetime? The town house had been his first purchase, and although he enjoyed living there, it had really been nothing more than a place to sleep. How else could he explain having lived there for seven years and never meeting Madge Sinclair?

Now *this* was a real house. This was a place where a man could feel as if he was indeed "king of his castle." This house, this particular pile of brick and lumber, could be a refuge from the hospital as well as a welcoming beacon that guided him home each night to his waiting family—to his waiting wife.

His family. Dr. and Mrs. Luke Manning and their children, Michael and Sarah.

Idly fingering a frond of a soft green fern that stood nearly as tall as he did, Luke congratulated himself yet again on his brilliant plan. He could see the positive changes in Michael and Sarah already. And the affection that showed in their eyes when they looked at him almost made up for the guarded expression in Emily's lovely brown eyes and the hesitancy in her voice when she spoke of their future.

He didn't love Emily Cornell; it was too soon to call what he felt for her love, but he did like and admire her. He liked her and, he had to admit, he was beginning to desire her. No, he *did* desire her. The feel of her hand, tucked confidently in his, the warmth of her soft body the times he had put his arm around her, even the look of surprise and pleasure in her eyes as he kissed her on the cheek whenever he saw her—all of these little things were adding up to one inevitable conclusion.

Emily Cornell was one sexy, desirable woman! One *very* desirable woman.

This might not be a marriage born of love, but it would not be long until it was a real marriage. Maybe deathless passion was not the only passion, and perhaps love came in many disguises.

Only time would tell.

He turned back to the bedroom and the waiting sales agent. "I asked for the cost of the model home as it stands, Ms. Woodward," he said firmly, decisively. "Now why don't you try adding up those numbers again—including the furniture and draperies."

Chapter Seven

SCORPIO: Muddle is the order of the day. Rushing your fences could prove hazardous. Honesty always the best policy, but, if not timely, not always the wisest. Children, love life, figure in scenario.

"I can't believe your house is sold already, Luke. When do the Myers want to move in? Michael, for pity's sake, sit still. I'm almost finished."

"About a month. They want to get in before school starts. For the sake of their kids, you know." Luke sat in his usual chair in Emily's small kitchen, watching in some amusement as she carefully clipped away a half inch of hair in the crucial area behind Michael's left ear. Emily's kitchen was more relaxing than being in his own living room with a cold beer and a good baseball game on the tube. He felt at ease, comfortable, and believed he had found the perfect way to end a long day at the hospital.

Emily was dressed for the warm weather, in a blue-and-white striped tank top and white shorts, her small, narrow feet bare, and Luke thought she looked like a little sailor girl who should be sunning herself on a secluded beach rather than standing in a kitchen, cutting hair.

Yes, she'd look at home on a beach, he decided, and it would be wonderful if they could go to the Jersey shore on their honeymoon. That vision evaporated as soon as it materialized, Luke remembering that theirs was not to be a conventional marriage, and that there would be no honeymoon.

Which was a pity. Emily would have looked great on that beach.

As he watched her work, Emily stuck the tip of her tongue in one corner of her mouth, much as Sarah did whenever she was concentrating on a project. Luke's smile turned into a wry grimace. But he didn't want to take Sarah to the beach.

Just Emily. Emily and him, alone. Getting to know each other. Moving beyond the admiration they had for each other, the mutual respect, the friendship, and into—what? Desire? Passion? Love?

"Ow, Mommy! You're pulling my hair!"

"No, I'm not, darling," Luke heard Emily answer in typical frazzled-mother tones. "But if you'd like me to—just so that you could tell me the difference—I'd be happy to oblige."

"No, that's okay," Michael assured her quickly, so that Luke and Emily exchanged knowing smiles—just like parents all over the world, wordlessly communicating with each other.

That silent communion, Luke decided, was a nice feeling.

He looked at the young boy who was soon to become his stepson. Michael sat perched on a high metal stool, both the floor beneath the chair and his own body protected by old shower curtains that Emily explained she'd saved to use for just this purpose.

Luke had offered to take Michael to one of the local barber shops but Emily had politely refused, saying it was silly to pay for a haircut when she had been cutting both Michael's and Sarah's hair since they were born. "After buying that house," she had added, smiling, "you should be grateful for my talent, not trying to talk me into spending more of your money."

She had seemed so serious, and he had already heard Emily's opinion of his impulsive purchase, his wedding gift to her, at great length. Luke hadn't bothered to explain that after spending what he had on the house, the price of a single haircut certainly wasn't going to bankrupt him.

Emily had been very vocal, extremely eloquent, on what she considered to be his high-handed maneuvering, agreeing to purchase the house and then telling her after the fact—although she seemed to be coming around. He hadn't known she had such a temper, but he had rather enjoyed being lectured on the fact that she was "a grown-up now, and capable of making decisions," on her own. He wouldn't be quick to forget what she had said.

Besides, as if to prove her point, she had immediately made an appointment with Ms. Woodward, during which she had gone over every item in the house with a figurative magnifying glass, pricing it, then keeping or discarding it from the list. From the pictures on the walls to the curtains in the family room to the plants in the master bathroom Emily had itemized, cataloged and either rejected or accepted everything, while Ms. Woodward had followed along through the house, her mouth slack, taking notes as quickly as possible.

It had been wonderful to see. It also had saved them several thousand dollars.

"Have you been over to the new house again today, General Cornell? I hear Ms. Woodward has asked to be transferred to their Houston office," he said, making faces at Michael, hoping to entertain him so that he wouldn't fidget while Emily was working.

"Not funny," she answered but then nodded, running a hand over Michael's hair, deliberately mussing it, then combing it again, scissors at the ready for any uneven lengths she might have missed. "We walked over this morning," she said, standing back to admire her job. "All the stage props the Realtor had set around are gone—the rented china and that unplayable grand piano in the living room. I still can't believe the piano was a prop. It looked so real."

"I know. All window dressing, but with nothing inside. I've known people like that, but never a piano." Once Emily had unclipped the shower curtain from Michael's shoulders, Luke stood and lifted the child off the stool. "There you go, tiger," he said, giving Michael's cheek a pat. "Looking good. It's nice to see your ears again."

"Now you'd better go change that shirt," Emily added as Michael turned to head outside. She took hold of him by the shoulders and gently steered him in the opposite direction. "Just in case some pieces of hair found their way down your collar."

As Luke put his hand on the back of the stool to replace it in the corner, Emily released Michael and took hold of Luke's arm, shaking her head. "Hold it, buster. You're next."

"*Me?*" Luke looked to the stool, then to the pink-flowered plastic shower curtain and lastly to the small, sharp scissors Emily was opening and closing not six inches from his nose. "I don't think so."

"Ah, but I do. You're beginning to look like Fred. What's the matter, Luke? Don't you trust me?" Emily smiled at him, a smile so innocent, so lacking in guile that he was sure she harbored plans to shave his head. "Believe me, I've been cutting hair for years and haven't ever drawn blood—yet."

Luke returned her smile, but didn't sit on the stool. They got along so well, it was sometimes hard to believe they were going to be married. They were such good friends. "You're cute when you're pretending to be lethal, Emily," he commented, leaning down to kiss her cheek. "But I think I'll pass."

"Dr. Manning? How come you do that?"

Both Emily and Luke turned to see that the young boy had not yet left the kitchen. "Why do I do what, Michael?"

Michael bobbed his head from side to side, pulling a face and rolling his eyes. Clearly he believed adults to be extremely dense. "You *know,* Dr. Manning," he said in an exasperated, singsong tone. "Why do you kiss Mommy like that? You said we're going to be married. Married people on television don't kiss like that. *Nobody* on the television show Aunt Madge watches in the afternoon kisses like that."

Emily began folding up the pink-flowered shower curtain, as if forgetting that she had planned to cut Luke's hair. Obviously Michael's question had embarrassed her. Heaven only knew Luke wasn't exactly comfortable with the boy's questions himself.

Luke crouched in front of Michael, taking hold of his arms. "Really, tiger? You know, I don't watch a lot of daytime television, so maybe you can help me out. How do those people kiss?"

The big brown pupils made another orbit inside Michael's eyes. "*You* know, Dr. Manning. They kiss on the mouth. The kisses are real sloppy, and they go on *forever,* and sometimes Aunt Madge sighs, like she thinks it's beautiful or something. Sarah thinks it's funny, but I think it's yicky."

Luke shot a look over his shoulder at Emily, who was making quite a production out of replacing the stool in the corner. "Do you want this one, or should I handle it?" he asked, praying she would jump into this pool of potential trouble somewhere along the line, or at least toss him some sort of lifeline that would help him navigate out of the deep end.

But Emily only put out her hands, palms facing him, and made pushing motions in his direction. "All yours, Doctor,'' she said before walking over to the sink and getting herself a glass of water. ''I wouldn't think to intrude on this man-to-man conversation.''

''Great. I ask for help and she tosses me an anchor.'' Luke mouthed the words under his breath before turning back to the waiting Michael. ''I thought kids watched *Sesame Street,* or spaceman cartoons. When did you start watching soap operas?''

''When we started going to Aunt Madge's house,'' Michael answered, ''but we only watch when it rains or it's too cold to go outside. We're supposed to have milk and cookies in the kitchen while her favorite one is on, but sometimes we get done early and go into the living room and watch with her. You see, Aunt Madge really likes the one that comes on just when I get home from school and never misses it. One of the guys on the show is a spy who sings sometimes—and there's this lady who doesn't know who she is, but thinks she's two other people and dresses up in old-fashioned clothes and hides in closets. It's really neat—except for when they kiss. After it's over we watch cartoons.''

''Ah, the wonders of nineties television,'' Luke said, sighing. ''Whatever happened to good books? But I guess we'll save that question for another time. You want to know about this kissing business right now, don't you, tiger?''

Michael nodded. ''Well, yeah. Me and Sarah—'' he looked up as Emily exaggeratedly cleared her throat, then continued, ''*Sarah and I* talked about it, and we think you should be kissing Mommy on the mouth. And hugging her. If we're getting married, that is. We really are, aren't we? 'Cause—'' he looked once more toward his mother "—*Sarah and I* sure do want us to."

"I see," Luke said, something about *mouths of babes* reverberating in his brain. "You're worried, are you, tiger? Worried that your mommy and I aren't really going to be married next month?"

Michael nodded once more, his wounded-puppy brown eyes huge and shiny, as if he was holding back tears. "We've got a new house and everything, and Mommy bought me a suit to wear to the wedding, but—" His words died away and he turned his head, as if eager to get himself out of both this conversation and the kitchen.

"But you want us to kiss," Luke ended for him.

Michael turned back, smiling. "Yeah, I guess so. And hug. Sarah says you oughta hug, the way Aunt Madge and Uncle Jim do when he comes home from work. And maybe call each other goofy names."

"I guess that's reasonable." Luke stood, looking toward Emily and wondering what Jim Sinclair called Madge when he was feeling romantic. Then again, maybe he didn't want to know. "What do you say, *sweetheart?*" he asked, grinning at her. "Shall we accommodate the children?"

Immediately, the blush Luke had grown to adore flew into Emily's cheeks. "This is silly," she said quickly, placing her water glass on the countertop and bending to fold up the second shower curtain. "Michael, you're being ridiculous. You're both being ridiculous—and I'm going to *murder* Madge!"

Luke knew Emily was nervous. Hell, he was nervous, too. He had come over here this evening to talk to Emily about a settlement date for buying the house, not to perform party tricks for an apprehensive six-year-old who watched too much television. But Michael *was* worried, and Luke wanted any fears the children might have nipped in the bud.

Besides, he had been looking for an excuse to kiss Emily "on the mouth." He had been looking for just such a reason since the day they had toured the model home and she had looked so "right" in the house he planned to make their home. The settlement date wasn't the reason he had come over. The real reason lay tucked in his shirt pocket, burning a hole there while he waited for the chance to be alone with Emily.

Not that he could tell her any of that. Emily had agreed to a marriage of, as the term went, "convenience." They had made a prenuptial agreement, not on paper, perhaps, but morally binding. She might not yet find it "convenient" that he had begun to look at her more in the role of wife than mother. Yet, how much could it hurt to give her a small hint of his changing feelings? As she had already commented—how else were they to do it? Send up flares?

Still looking at Emily, Luke asked, "Michael? Where's your sister?"

"Upstairs, playing with her dolls or something. Are you gonna do it, Dr. Manning? Huh? Are you gonna do it?"

"Michael—"

Luke cut Emily off in mid-protest. "Go upstairs to Sarah, Michael. Give us ten minutes alone, and then your mother and I will see if we can't convince you that we are indeed going to be married."

Michael was barely out of the room before Emily attacked. "I don't believe this! You're going to kiss me because of something Michael saw on one of Madge's soap operas?"

"And hug you, Emily, *sweetheart*. Let's not forget the hug." Luke advanced toward her so that she backed up against the sink. "It will make the children relax. Besides, I think we got off lucky. They could have thought I was a singing spy and you were an amnesiac suffering from a split personality who wears old-fashioned clothes and hides in closets."

His attempt at a joke seemed to take the edge off her anger, if not her fear. She picked up a dishcloth and began wiping the already-clean countertop. "Michael does seem to need reassurance. It's just that things are moving so fast—"

Luke stepped closer to her, putting his hand on hers, stilling her movement. God, she was trembling. "Emily," he said, waiting until she turned to face him, "if it makes you feel any better, I'm just as nervous as you. We have been moving pretty quickly—in many ways—except for this one. I think perhaps we should practice before the children come in here."

"Practice?" Emily's eyes were suddenly as huge and round as Michael's. "You mean we should practice kissing? Why? I was married, you were engaged. We're adults. We've both kissed people before."

Luke slipped his arms around her slim waist, drawing her closer, feeling her fingers tremble as she laid her hands on his bare forearms, not to push him away, but more as if she needed to hold on to him in order to maintain her balance.

She smelled of soap and sunshine again, the mingled scents immediately recognized by what he had begun to think of as his treacherous baser instincts—most of which were located somewhere deep in the pit of his stomach. The passion he had believed lost to him, and better left behind, stirred once more in his blood.

"Emily, we need to talk," he said, surprising himself with the sudden seriousness of his tone. "I've been thinking—"

Now she did push him away. "I knew it!" she said, leaning back against the sink. "I knew this wouldn't work. Wanting a family is one thing, Luke, but giving up your freedom is quite another. You're a young man. You should have been looking for a woman to love, and *then* proposed marriage. You should have had your own children—be looking forward to having your own children. I've been there, Luke. I've had the husband and the marriage and the children—the whole enchilada. My life now is working and taking care of those children—and wondering if I can afford to buy a new washing machine. Love was the last thing on my mind when I met you. But you were cheated two years ago."

She turned her back on him, looking out the window over the sink, staring at the backyard. "You can leave, Luke. I'll explain to the children."

He put his hands on her shoulders, chuckling softly as he turned her around to face him. " 'The whole enchilada?' You sure can jump to conclusions, can't you, sweetheart? How long have you been worried that I might change my mind?"

She avoided his eyes, biting on her bottom lip.

"You spoke of the benefits of our arrangement being rather one-sided," he continued as another thought sobered him. "Do you still believe you're getting the best part of our bargain—that I'm cheating myself? Unless it's something else. Unless I'm looking at this from the wrong angle. Emily—is it still too soon after Mark's death?"

She looked up at him quizzically. "Mark? What does Mark have to do with any of this? I thought you changed your mind. I thought you wanted to call off the marriage. Luke—I'm lost! *What* are we talking about?"

Once again he had brought up her late husband's name, and once again Emily had deflected him. She must have loved him very much if even the sound of his name was painful to her.

Then, as what she had said penetrated his brain, Luke relaxed, realizing they had been talking—and thinking—at cross-purposes.

"I don't want to call off our marriage, Emily," he explained, gently rubbing his unusually sensitized hands up and down her bare arms. Her soft, touchable bare arms.

"You don't?"

"No, I don't. Quite the opposite. I guess I hadn't really given the intimate side of our marriage a lot of thought—didn't think through much of anything, actually, but when we toured the house and you picked out your bedroom, well, I didn't like it. I know we agreed to go slow, Emily, but I think I want to send up that flare now, if it's all right with you. I want to make ours a real marriage—from the very beginning.''

Her eyes grew wide. "But—but what about our agreement?"

He turned away from her, disgusted with himself. "Damn, Emily, I'm sorry. When I think about it, when I'm with you, it all seems so normal. But when I *say* it, it sounds so one-sided again, so damn selfish!"

"No, Luke," she answered, her tone vehement. "No, you don't sound either one-sided or selfish. You sound like a normal man. It's our arrangement that's abnormal. Platonic marriages only work in fiction, like on Madge's soap operas. Although, now that I think of it, according to Michael, there couldn't be any platonic marriages on soap operas, either, not with the amount of sloppy kissing and hugging Michael talked about seeing."

Luke gazed into her eyes—her beautiful, soft brown eyes. In fact, he decided, Emily was the most beautiful woman he had ever seen. And the most desirable. If only he could tell her that he believed he was falling in love with her. But it was too soon—or maybe it was too late. Damn! If only they could go back to the beginning and start again, and do it right this time!

"So you're breaking the engagement," he said fatalistically.

Emily shook her head, smiling. "No. I can't do that, Luke. The kids would never forgive me," she said in a teasing voice. "I don't know if you caught it, but Michael asked if 'we' are still getting married. To the kids, this is a real group project."

She hesitated for a moment, then seemed to gather her courage to say whatever else was on her mind. "But I would like some time to get used to this latest idea. For both of us. And—and maybe if you could court me? Just a little, if you don't think I'm being silly?"

"Court you?"

Emily frowned. "Yes, Luke, I think I want you to court me. I know it's an old-fashioned term, but I kinda like it."

"Court you," Luke repeated, smiling as he realized that Emily already knew what he had just discovered—that they had gone about this whole thing backward. They had agreed to marry, and now, if Emily got her wish, they were going to date. "You mean, like taking you to dinner and out dancing?"

"And bringing me flowers and calling me 'dopey names,'" she added, laughing. "A woman may like big houses and beautiful furniture and financial security, but she'll take romance over all of that anyday."

So would he, Luke realized, his heart suddenly light. So would he. "Well, we only have three weeks before the wedding," he said. "It'll be close, but I think we can make it. Maybe—" he said, reaching into his shirt pocket to withdraw the small velvet jeweler's box he had nearly forgotten he'd brought with him "—maybe we should start with this? After all, you can't wear a house."

He opened the box, revealing the perfect marquis diamond set in a slim gold band. "It's probably not your size, but the jeweler assured me we can have it fitted when we go to choose our wedding rings."

Emily was bent over the box, her fingers outstretched as if she longed to snatch up the ring, although she didn't. She just stood there, staring at it, not saying anything.

He hadn't planned to buy the engagement ring. For one thing, Emily still wore the thick gold band from her first marriage. It wasn't until he had seen the diamond while he was downtown and passed by a jeweler's window, that he had realized how much it bothered him that Mark's ring was still on her finger.

"I didn't know. I mean, I've thought about it. I suppose it's only natural for a woman to *think* about it—to wonder if the man she is going to marry wants to wear a ring, wants to advertise the fact that he's married—but I never really *believed*, and Mark never—Luke, do you really plan to wear a wedding ring?" Emily asked, still looking at the diamond.

"Everywhere except in the operating room, Emily. I thought you had me all figured out—I'm a sucker for tradition. Always have been. I guess it goes right along with this craving I have for a wife and family."

Believing she'd never pick up the ring, Luke removed it from the box and placed it in her palm. "I looked at other rings, other styles, but there was something about this one that reminded me of you. Do you like it?"

She looked up at him, her eyes shining with tears. Happy tears. Or at least he hoped they were happy tears. "Like it? Oh, Luke—I love it! It's the most beautiful thing I've ever seen. Thank you. Thank you so much!''

Her obvious pleasure stirred something deep inside him, a warmth not unmingled with passion, and he felt good, very good. He liked pleasing Emily. He liked to see her face light up with pleasure. His feelings for her were not just of friendship, or of physical passion. His feelings for her went deeper than that. As a matter of fact, he suddenly realized he could make trying to please Emily his life's work and never grow tired of her smiles.

The moment was wonderful, but it rapidly grew awkward. Luke wanted to place the ring on Emily's finger, but he couldn't ask her to remove Mark's ring. That, he was sure, was something she would want to do privately, for it would be the final severing of her first marriage, the last official act meant to put the past behind her and move into the future.

Their future.

He handed her the box and, just as he had supposed, she replaced the ring in its specially formed bed of blue velvet, then closed the lid. He had expected this, but he knew he could not hide his disappointment.

"I, um, I think the kids will be downstairs soon," Emily remarked, sliding the velvet box into the pocket of her shorts. "You, um, you mentioned something about practicing?''

The overture was spoken in a small, faintly timid voice, but it was an overture, and Luke, remembering their talk of half a loaf being better than none, forced a smile onto his face and slipped his arms around

Emily's waist. She laid her hands on his forearms, smiling up into his eyes.

"Yes, I believe I did mention something like that," he said, taking a small step closer to her, so that their bodies touched, hip to thigh. Immediately his nerve endings tingled; he felt as if he had just been given a small electrical shock. "I think we're already beginning to get the hang of the hugging part of it. Do you think we're ready for some 'yicky' kissing?"

Emily took a deep breath, then nodded. "Ready when you are, friend," she whispered, repositioning her hands on his shoulders as she raised herself up on tiptoe. "I hear it's like riding a bicycle. Once learned, you never really forget how, no matter how long it has been since you've been on a bike."

So saying, Emily closed her eyes, her lips pursed in anticipation—at least Luke hoped it was anticipation. He swallowed hard, feeling as nervous as he had at his cousin's thirteenth birthday party—the one where they had played spin the bottle and he'd had to go behind a curtain and kiss Maryjane O'Hara. It had been his first kiss, his first test, and he had known that to fail would mean his life would be over. If he goofed up, Maryjane—who was known to be "experienced"—would tell everyone how inept he had been and he might as well move to the South Pole and live with the penguins.

Emily's kitchen might not be his cousin's recreation room, but it was a testing ground nonetheless. And Luke knew that, once more, he couldn't afford to fail.

Gently cupping Emily's chin in one hand, he ran a fingertip along her bottom lip, easing it smooth from its pucker, then watched as Emily's eyes opened wide in either pleasure or shock.

Luke silently prayed it was pleasure.

Lowering his head, he slanted it slightly to the left and lightly caught Emily's bottom lip between his before sliding the tip of his tongue along the moist skin inside, her soft sigh flowing into his as he took complete possession of her mouth.

He felt a rush, a sensation of pleasure liberally mixed with pain, begin deep inside him, and he gathered her close, closer, glorying in her sweetness, her gentle vulnerability, her near-innocence as her hands fluttered for a moment just above his shoulders and then settled trustingly against him once more.

"All right, Mom! Way to go!" Michael congratulated from somewhere behind them, and suddenly Emily was gone, mumbling something about needing to go to the basement and put some laundry in the dryer, leaving Luke to wonder if he had just imagined that they had kissed very much like two people in love.

Late that night, after Luke had gone and the children had been bathed and put to sleep, Emily lay in her own bed, remembering how she had compared kissing a man to riding a bicycle.

She looked up and watched the reflected glow of the streetlamp dance on the ceiling as a breeze ruffled the leaves of the tree just outside her bedroom window.

"A bicycle," she mused aloud, wondering at her own naïveté. Silly girl. Kissing Luke, being kissed by

Luke, was nothing like riding a bicycle. A stomach-clenching, nerve-tingling, heart-pounding ride on a world-class roller coaster seemed to be an eminently better vehicle of comparison—and she didn't think she'd ever been on one in her entire life.

Emily closed her eyes, longing to relive the moments she had spent locked in Luke's arms before the children had reappeared, Michael interrupting them with his triumphant exclamation. After hiding in the basement for five minutes like some giddy teenager, she had joined the three of them in the living room, then spent the remainder of the evening playing a board game on the floor, Sarah sitting close behind Emily, guarding her, as if she didn't want Luke to come near her mommy.

Emily still didn't know what she had expected when Luke's head had dipped toward hers, his mouth finding hers in what had begun as a gentle, tentative joining of their lips. But whatever she had expected, she had not been prepared for the immediate, intensely physical reaction that had raced through her body, causing her to cling to him with both hands, fearful she might fall off the edge of the world if he let her go.

Mark had given Emily her first kiss, her only "man and woman" kisses. Her reaction to her late husband's lovemaking was, she realized, the only comparison she had to hold up to the feelings that had shot straight to the core of her being when Luke's lips had so reverently touched hers, when, a few moments later, he had deepened that kiss.

And now she knew. Comparing Luke's kisses to Mark's was like comparing a Rolls Royce to a kiddie car. Other than the fact that both had four wheels, they had absolutely nothing in common.

She looked across the room to where the velvet ring box sat on the dresser. The diamond ring still nestled inside, awaiting the moment she would remove Mark's ring.

But Emily couldn't remove the ring just yet. She knew that Luke wanted her to, but she just couldn't, and not because of any lingering emotional attachment. Thanks to bodily changes caused by her two pregnancies, the ring was now too small to fit over her knuckle, not that she would have told Luke that. It was just too silly. But as soon as possible she would go to a jeweler and have it cut off, then save the pieces for her children. She owed Mark that.

But she didn't want to think about Mark now. Mark belonged to her past. She wanted to think about Luke, and about the kiss they had shared.

Apart from her growing love for Luke Manning the man, she had been quick to recognize that Luke was also a handsome specimen, an eminently sensual, desirable man. A man women were instinctively drawn to, wondering what it would be like to be held by him, kissed by him, made love to by him.

Even the fact that he had seemed to eschew such a romantic involvement, craving nothing more than a ready-made family and a "friendly" marriage, hadn't been enough to keep Emily from falling in love with him and from dreaming that someday he would want theirs to be a real marriage.

And now he did.

Wasn't that wonderful?

Indeed it was.

It was *eminently* wonderful.

If he desired her, could love be far behind?

Emily snuggled down beneath the covers, a hand pressed to her mouth to cover a sudden attack of giggles.

Chapter Eight

AUGUST 10:
YOUR DAILY ASTROLOGICAL FORECAST

SCORPIO: Your love of pomp, ceremony, indulged. Attention continues to center on marital situation, possible change of residence. Old friends resurface, bringing possible problems. Be careful, or you could jeopardize newfound happiness.

Luke hadn't been this nervous since...since...Lord! He couldn't remember ever being this nervous. At a prearranged signal from the organist, he walked out of the anteroom and stood in front of the altar of the small university chapel, the collar of his new white shirt too tight, his heart pounding unevenly, his palms clammy, waiting for the moment his bride would walk down the short aisle, Sarah leading the way.

Michael stood beside him, acting as best man, his hands stuck deep in his pockets as he rocked back and forth on his heels, craning his neck to see the guests.

There were not many. Neither Emily nor Luke had any close family, and the few cousins and friends that were already seated would not have been enough to justify performing the wedding in a church. Besides, the chapel was perfect: intimate, richly furnished with mahogany pews and velvet draperies, with a lovely stained-glass window behind the altar, the whole set off by brass stands holding fat, white candles, their flames flickering against the paneled walls.

A twilight wedding ceremony performed in this chapel couldn't be viewed as anything but permanent. Binding. For better or worse. Till death did them part.

"I thought you said Mommy was coming in next, but she's not. Who's that?" Michael said in a stage whisper, tugging on Luke's navy blue suit jacket as he pointed at the couple just entering the chapel. "Wow! Is he in movies?"

Luke didn't have to look to know who Michael had seen. Only one man he knew could make such an instant impression upon a six-year-old boy.

Max Rafferty had just come into the chapel—or come onstage. With Max, bless him, it was much the same thing. The man couldn't help it. His frank friendliness, winning personality and classic good looks prevented him from moving about unnoticed in the middle of a thousand people, let alone in this small chapel.

And, with the strikingly beautiful Julia on his arm, Max's entrance wouldn't have gone unnoticed if this same chapel had suddenly burst into flames.

Julia. Luke had told Emily the truth when he'd said he and the Raffertys exchanged Christmas cards, although he hadn't yet shown her the picture of Sean. They had even spoken on the telephone from time to time, especially while Julia had been pregnant. Max's phone calls for reassurance every time his wife exhibited perfectly normal symptoms of pregnancy amused Luke even as they had sometimes made him wistful for what might have been if Max hadn't come back into Julia's life two years ago.

Perhaps that was when the seed had been planted. Perhaps it was the birth of Julia and Max's child, Sean, almost six months ago that had spurred him into deciding that he, too, wanted a family. Could their obvious happiness have caused him to approach Emily with the notion of this marriage, the idea that he, too, deserved a little happiness?

Luke slanted a look toward the aisle, and Julia rewarded him with a small wave and a wide smile before allowing Max to guide her into a pew. She was even more lovely than Luke remembered. Two years of a happy marriage and motherhood had only added to her beauty, slightly softening the sleek, sophisticated, faintly brittle exterior he had fought so hard to penetrate, the shield she had built around her emotions after her breakup with Max.

Luke had "courted" Julia, gently wooing her, carefully peeling away every barrier she had thrown up to protect herself from being hurt—winning her only to lose her to Max.

No, that wasn't true. Luke knew he had never really had Julia, not all of her. She had loved him, yes, but she had not been in love with him. She had decided to "settle," to accept that half loaf his proposal of marriage had offered. She had been unwilling to

open herself to the sort of burning passion she had felt
with Max, unwilling to open herself once more to the
pain that she had felt when their marriage had disin-
tegrated.

Luke turned back to the altar, realizing that he had
attempted to do the same thing Julia had done—but
with a twist. He had decided to "settle" for that same
sort of half loaf, refusing to see what was in front of
his face. Unwilling to recognize his feelings for Emily
for what they were, unwilling to give another name
besides friendship to those feelings, unwilling to give
in to the passion again, afraid of the heat, fearful of
being burned once more.

Max, a firm believer in the Zodiac, would have said
that, both being Scorpios, it was a foregone conclusion that Julia and Luke should have the same reaction to being hurt.

But Luke didn't believe in the Zodiac. He had simply told himself that he had "settled" for friendship,
for respect, for a mutual admiration. He had tried to
convince himself that he had "settled" for a ready-
made family, a storybook house, a pleasant companion, shared goals and a lifetime that no longer included frozen dinners for one and a too-quiet house
when he came home at night.

And then they had gotten to know each other, after
the fact. After the proposal. After the arrangement
had been agreed upon, the ridiculous notion that two
adults could live under the same roof and not con-
summate their marriage. How could he ever have believed such a plan to be rational? Thank God they had
never committed such a ridiculous prenuptial agreement to paper.

When they had kissed, on that fateful night only three weeks ago, Luke had known once and for all that his carelessly conceived plans had gone straight out the door. And good riddance to them. What would he have done if Emily had not reacted so sweetly, sliding her arms around his neck, opening her lips to him, welcoming his touch, trading friendship for passion in that one blinding instant of revelation?

Yet three weeks had passed and they had not discussed the implications of that eye-opening, pact-destroying kiss. Nor had they advanced beyond it. How could they, when Luke hadn't had a free moment to so much as take Emily out for a candlelight dinner or an evening of dancing?

First Sarah, then Michael, had come down with miserable summer colds, keeping Emily busy for a week, before she declared herself willing to leave them with Madge for an evening. As a matter of fact, the only time he had seen her alone that week was when he had dropped off his guest list for the wedding.

With reservations made at a local restaurant the following Friday night, Luke had been ready to walk down to Emily's house to pick her up, when his beeper had gone off, summoning him to the hospital for an emergency. A bus filled with young campers had gone off the turnpike and into a ditch, injuring more than twenty of the children. Many of them had required surgery, and Luke was already covering for another surgeon who was on vacation overseas.

The campers, adding to his already-heavy surgical schedule—elective surgeries he had hoped to get out of the way before the wedding—had kept Luke at the hospital for endless hours, and he had spent several nights sleeping on that cracked leather couch in his office.

The last ten days had been filled with packing and moving everyone's belongings to the new house, disposing of most of their old furniture and attending settlement meetings for all three houses.

Each passing day, each new crisis, each hour spent away from his soon-to-be wife, had increased Luke's desire, his passion.

But they seemed to have had the opposite effect on Emily. She had grown curiously shy again, almost as if she was afraid of him, afraid of the day when all the rushing and juggling of chores would be over and they were together in the new house—the children safely tucked up at Madge's for the night—alone with each other as man and wife.

Luke frowned as he remembered that it had taken Emily three whole days to remove her wedding ring and replace it with the marquis diamond. He never asked her why she had delayed in making the transition. Their good-night kisses at her front door, the only time they ever seemed to be alone, were too precious to interrupt with questions about her old wedding ring.

Luke was suddenly aware that the organist had begun the "Bridal March" and the guests were standing, everyone facing the doorway to the vestibule. He turned with them, Michael stepping in front of him to get a better view of his sister and mother as they came down the aisle.

His gaze first touched on Julia, who was dressed in one of her trademark silk ensembles, this one of faintest pink blush, her long, dark hair drawn up in a feature-softening Gibson-girl style and secured in a topknot. She did look wonderful. As he watched, Max rested a hand on his wife's shoulder, drawing her close and whispering something in her ear, so that she turned and kissed his cheek.

Luke smiled, glad he had invited the Raffertys. Julia was obviously happy. And he was happy for her. Genuinely happy. Her appearance today had given him his last bit of proof, not that he'd needed it. It was true. The past was gone.

It was time to look to the future.

And then Sarah appeared at the top of the aisle, dressed in softest yellow. Her small face was solemn as she stepped carefully onto the white cloth runner, reaching her hand into the basket she carried and scattering one yellow rose petal at a time in front of her as she progressed up the aisle toward Luke.

When she reached him she looked up and smiled, obviously thrilled to have performed so well, then walked to the other side of the aisle.

He winked at her, unbelievably proud of his soon-to-be new daughter, then turned to watch Emily's entrance.

And if Luke hadn't already been in love with Emily Cornell before she walked toward him down the aisle—her expression just as solemn as Sarah's had been, her chin held high, her butter yellow tea-length gown flattering her finely formed figure, an absurd wisp of a hat perched jauntily atop her soft brown curls—he knew he was lost now.

Completely and utterly lost.

He moved through the motions of the marriage ceremony as if in a dream, knowing he would probably never remember anything more than brief scenes...snippets of seeing Sarah tugging possessively at her mother's skirt...Michael's sudden attack of hiccups that had set the minister chuckling as he performed a reading from the Bible...the sound of Madge Sinclair's lusty sobs as the vows were exchanged.

Mostly he would remember the slight tremor in his voice as he pledged his troth...Emily's sure-voiced recitation of her vows as she stared up at him with her lovely brown eyes...the sweet smell of the yellow tea roses in her hair...the even-sweeter taste of her lips a scant second after the minister pronounced, "You may kiss the bride."

But more than anything else, Luke knew he would always remember his private, unspoken vow—the one in which he promised himself he would do everything in his power, today, forever, to be worthy of Emily's trust in him.

"A toast!" Max Rafferty announced, rising from his chair in the restaurant's small private dining room that had been chosen for the reception dinner. "To Dr. and Mrs. Luke Manning. 'May the road rise to meet you. May the wind be always at your backs. May the sun shine warm upon your faces, the rains fall soft upon your fields...and may God hold you all in the palm of His hand.'" He held up his glass. "To Luke and Emily! Live long and prosper!"

"Hear! Hear!" the male guests echoed, raising their glasses as Emily blinked away sudden tears. "Dr. and Mrs. Luke Manning." It had a nice ring to it, she decided, peering up at her husband from beneath her lashes.

The plain gold band on her finger, already joined by the marquis diamond, felt strangely heavy on her hand, and almost too shiny, too new, to be believed. But it was true. She was Mrs. Luke Manning. Emily Manning. Luke and Emily. Emily and Luke. "Till death do you part."

The wedding ceremony had been brief but poignant, with Sarah and Michael serving as their attendants. Michael's eyes had grown wide when he realized he had forgotten which pocket of his new suit held the rings. That little fright had probably caused his attack of hiccups, poor darling.

Bless Luke for not minding—for Emily had heard his chuckle and knew he wasn't angry with the child.

Madge Sinclair, taking on the role of mother of the bride, had sniffled audibly into her handkerchief throughout the exchange of vows, before standing at the back of the chapel once the ceremony was over, telling anyone who would listen that she "knew the moment I saw them together that it was a match made in Heaven."

Emily barely remembered being in the receiving line at the rear of the chapel. She had still been floating muzzily as she relived Luke's solemnly spoken vows and the way he had looked so deeply into her eyes as he had said them, his handsome face so serious that she had felt tears stinging the backs of her eyes.

And then there was their kiss at the end of the ceremony. That memory lingered also, as did the feel of Luke's mouth against hers and the unspoken vow they had exchanged with that kiss almost before the minister had prompted them to do so.

She had glowed as she stood beside her new husband in the receiving line. She had been able to actually feel the warmth of that happy glow—right up until the moment Luke had slipped his arm around her and said, "Emily, I'd like you to meet Julia and Max Rafferty."

Emily hadn't wanted to look, hadn't been ready to see Luke's old love, the woman who had spurned him for another and sent Luke into a shell for two long years. The woman who had so shattered him by her defection that he had decided to settle for a "comfortable" marriage rather than look for another fire that could burn as brightly—no, darn it all, *brighter!*—than the one he and Julia had shared.

And then there was the matter of jealousy. Mark had been jealous, unreasonably so, ever since he had slipped that dime-store friendship ring on her finger when they were in the eighth grade. Emily refused to allow herself to feel jealousy for Julia's past relationship with Luke, for his love for the woman. Jealousy, she knew, could tear the heart out of love, and turn even the most longed-for emotion into dust.

Before she could raise her eyes, before she could bring herself to look into the eyes of her nemesis, the woman whose name—so unbelievably—had appeared on Luke's list of invited guests just in time to keep her from admitting to him that she had fallen in love with him, Emily was enveloped in a silken, perfumed embrace.

"Emily!" Julia Rafferty had exclaimed, kissing her cheek before stepping back, a wide smile lighting her beautiful face. "What a pleasure it is to meet you! You're everything Luke has said, and more. And your children! What perfect little angels! I cried all the way through the ceremony!"

Emily smiled now as she remembered looking at Julia, seeing the tall, sleekly sophisticated woman and the handsome, tawny-haired man at her side. Julia's eyes were indeed moist, and her expression was openly friendly and devoid of any traces of superiority. The woman was truly happy for her!

And then Max, the man who had just taken it upon himself to toast the newlyweds, had kissed her cheek, offering her his best wishes before congratulating her groom on his extreme good luck.

How could she be cool to these two people who obviously had nothing but kindness in their hearts for her? Besides, if Julia and Max hadn't gotten back together, she would not be standing here today as Mrs. Luke Manning!

Yes, Emily had found it impossible to hold either Rafferty at arm's length, as she had thought to do on all the nights she had lain awake since mailing the invitation, sure she would hate both of them on sight. They were so friendly, so genuinely happy for Luke, so very willing to accept Emily and the children.

Emily nodded to Max Rafferty now before lifting her glass. She touched its rim to Luke's glass and sipped at the champagne while smiling into his eyes— the two of them immediately drawn into their own private world, a place where the wedding guests had all said their farewells and gone away, leaving them gloriously alone—and willed this moment to go on forever.

Luke broke eye contact first, which Emily considered to be a good thing, for she knew she was blushing. He stood, causing all the guests to once more rise from their chairs, and turned to hold out his glass as he saluted his bride. "To my wife, Emily Manning," he said, his eyes never leaving hers, "who has given me more today than any man could ever want. Her hand, her promise and Michael and Sarah—my new family. Emily, once more I give you *my* hand and *my* promise—the promise that I will spend the rest of my life doing everything in my power to be certain you will never regret this day."

"Hear! Hear!" the men called again, soon to be drowned out by the clinking of knives against the wineglasses—the tinkling sound growing toward a tinny crescendo in the age-old custom signaling that the guests would like the bride and groom to kiss.

Emily, sure her cheeks were flaming, allowed Luke to take her hand, helping her to rise. "Madge started this, of course," she commiserated as Luke put a finger beneath her chin, raising her face to his. "I'll understand if you don't want to put on a show for her, honestly—"

That's as far as she got before Luke swooped down to capture her mouth with his, sweeping her tightly into his arms while Madge and her husband, Jim, led the cheering and general well-wishing that seemed to have been prompted by their performance.

When Luke finally released her—and to Emily it seemed that at least two seasons had passed before he did—she subsided into her chair, unable to think of a thing to say. Luke had said it all with his kiss, without uttering a word.

They had met through her children. They had become engaged in an act of friendship, a mutual longing for a complete family. And now they had married, and their friendship was growing into an undeniable passion.

She smiled, not outwardly, but secretly, deep in her heart. Respect. Friendship. And tonight, very soon—passion.

Could declarations of love be far behind? She turned to look at Luke, her limbs melting as she traced his darkly handsome, clearly chiseled profile with her eyes.

Love.

So far that word had been spoken only in their vows—"to love and to cherish."

But soon, perhaps even as soon as tonight, they would feel free to speak that word again.

Emily felt Luke's hand on hers under the table, gloried in the reassuring pressure of his flesh upon hers even as he turned away to talk to a gray-haired man she recognized as one of the directors she had met at the dinner dance.

She allowed Sarah to climb onto her lap, soft blond curls pressing against her breast as the weary child closed her eyes and sucked on her thumb in a well-known signal that meant it was past her bedtime.

Poor baby. It had been a long day for the four-year-old who had dissolved into tears more than once, overwhelmed by all the ceremony, all the strange faces that had come into her orbit, cooing over her petite prettiness, complimenting her on her fine performance as flower girl and maid of honor.

Michael appeared beside Emily's chair a moment later, his suit jacket discarded, his tie askew, one shirttail somehow outside his trousers. "Mom? Is it all right that I ate two ice creams? Aunt Madge says to tell you she'll take us home with her now, 'cause Sarah looks tired. I think I want to go now, too. My stomach doesn't feel so good."

Luke must have heard, for he excused himself from the gray-haired man and pulled Michael onto his lap. "What's the matter, tiger? Too much wedding?"

"I guess so," Michael answered as Emily dipped the corner of a linen napkin into a water glass and dabbed at the evidence of his dessert that clung to the corners of his mouth. "Besides, Aunt Madge says it's time we left you guys alone. Mom? Why do you want to be alone? I thought we were married now. Don't you want me and Sarah anymore?"

Sarah's thumb was quickly ejected from her mouth as she turned her head into Emily's shoulder, her little arms clasped tightly about her mother's neck. "I don't want to go, Mommy! I don't want to go with Aunt Madge!" she cried. "I want to go to our new house with you and Michael and Fred."

"And Dr. Manning?" Emily prompted.

"Does he hafta come?" Sarah grimaced, then sighed. "Okay. Him too, I guess. But, please, Mommy, I want to be with you."

Luke smiled at Emily, who couldn't see anything funny about her predicament. She felt torn between her children and her new husband and, Lord help her, at the moment she was wishing those children straight into the back seat of Madge Sinclair's station wagon.

Yesterday she was a mother. Tomorrow she would be a mother again. But today—tonight—she was a bride. Tonight she was going to take a leisurely bubble bath in that glorious tub, tie her hair up with a white satin ribbon, slip into the scandalously expensive lace peignoir she had bought on impulse last week—and become a wife.

Couldn't Luke see that? Didn't Luke want to be a husband?

Obviously not.

"Emily?" he prompted, turning up Michael's chin so that she could see his wounded-puppy brown eyes, the eyes that had never failed to cut straight to her heart—and her motherly feelings of guilt. "What do you think?"

Emily averted her gaze, as Luke's eyes now seemed to be pleading with her, as well. He didn't want to know what she thought. *She* didn't want to think about her thoughts. What sort of mother was she? How could she be jealous of her own children?

What could she do? What could she say? "Sorry, kids, but I have other plans for tonight and they sure as heck don't include you" didn't just sound selfish, it sounded desperate. Besides, it was obvious that Luke wasn't all that concerned about having the children with them, and this wasn't either the time or the place to point out that her sweet, darling children were engaging in a power struggle with their new stepfather.

Maybe it would be better this way—better if they eased themselves into the marriage and into the marriage bed. But better for whom? Luke? Emily? *Sarah?*

"I guess it will be four for breakfast," Emily murmured, capitulating, forcing her lips to curve into a smile.

Luke rewarded her with his own smile, only she was disappointed to see it, sure his was not forced. "Five, Emily. You, Sarah, Michael, Fred and then me. You did notice who came dead last in Sarah's pecking order?" he teased, tickling Sarah's ribs so that the child's tears turned to giggles. "Emily, I'm crushed. Why didn't you tell me you guys were marrying me for my sheepdog?"

Emily smiled once more, hoping Luke didn't notice that she was doing her best to overcome a sudden, strong urge to strangle the man she had just married.

When it came to bad ideas, Luke was beginning to believe he had cornered the market.

He had believed a man loved, really loved, only once in his life. Bad idea.

He had proposed marriage to a woman he barely knew, promising respect and friendship and only a nebulous plan for a more total commitment sometime in the future. Another lousy idea.

He had then proceeded to prove his first assumption incorrect and his proposal inane by falling madly in love with his bride—not that he'd bothered to share that little piece of information with her as yet.

Falling in love had not been a bad idea in itself. It had been wonderful, actually—unexpected, yet totally welcome—but he had gone about the entire business backward. It was going to take a lot of time, and some careful convincing, to prove to Emily that he had indeed fallen in love with her and that he was not ready to succumb to his desire merely because of her proximity or, even worse, animal passion.

And now he had compounded all of his bad ideas, drawn them all up into one huge, unwieldy ball and stuffed them inside the worst idea of all.

Why had he suggested they bring the children along to the new house on their wedding night? Their short, twenty-four-hour honeymoon?

What had he been drinking? What had he been thinking?

Luke prowled the family room, his jacket and tie discarded, a drink in his hand, clinking the ice against the sides of the glass as he looked toward the kitchen yet again, checking the clock that hung above the sink. Emily and the children had been upstairs for over an hour, Sarah refusing to go to sleep unless her mother lay down in the extra twin bed in her new room.

There might be monsters under the bed, Sarah had proposed, glaring at Luke as if she hated him, blamed him for taking her away from her old bedroom—for taking her mother away.

For *trying* to take her mother away, Luke thought, putting down the glass without tasting its contents. Considering the fact that it was nearing eleven o'clock and there was still no sign of Emily, it looked as if Sarah had won the first round in what he now realized to be a battle of wills.

"Dr. Manning?"

Luke turned to see Michael standing just inside the kitchen, his pajama collar turned up and one leg of his pajama bottoms hiked above his knee. "Hi-ya, tiger," he said, beckoning the child to come into the family room. "What's the matter? Have the monsters sublet in your room?'' He shook his head, knowing Michael couldn't understand his sarcasm. ''Never mind. Did you have a nightmare?''

Michael frowned, then shook his head. ''Sarah's a baby. There's no such things as monsters. Except maybe alligators, and they only come after you in the bathtub. But she's sleeping now, Sarah and Mommy both. I looked before I came downstairs.''

The child frowned again. ''Dr. Manning, I've been thinking—what am I supposed to call you now?''

Luke winced. *Usurper* might be a good term, if he could believe Sarah knew the meaning of the word. *Jackass* might be another one, considering the fact that his wife of a few hours was upstairs in a bedroom with her daughter, sound asleep, rather than preparing herself for a wedding night spent in the arms of her new husband.

Not that it mattered very much either way. Emily was probably so angry with him at the moment that their wedding night was already ruined.

''Come here, tiger,'' Luke said, motioning for Michael to join him on the couch. When the boy hopped onto the cushions, his expression alert, Luke tried to recall what Emily had said about how much Michael remembered of his father. It couldn't be much. He had wanted to discuss this business of names, of loyalties, of remembrances of Mark Cornell, but Emily never seemed to want to discuss Mark and he hadn't thought it a good idea to push her.

But now, while Emily was upstairs—either sleeping or sulking—Michael was asking the question Luke had been alternately dreading and anticipating. ''I don't know, tiger," he said at last. "What do you want to call me?"

Michael shrugged, his thin shoulders nearly sliding out of the gaping top of his pajamas. "Luke?" he suggested at last. "That's what Mommy calls you."

Indeed it was. Luke hid his disappointment behind a smile. "Then Luke it is," he agreed, assisting the boy off the couch. "That was simple, wasn't it? Do you want a drink of water before you go back to bed?"

"No thanks, Dr.—I mean, *Luke,*" Michael answered, his little face so sad Luke was suddenly sure he had just been put to some sort of test—and had failed miserably. "G'night."

"Sleep tight, tiger," Luke answered, watching the boy go before picking up his drink again, tamping down the urge to send the glass crashing into the cold hearth.

The euphoria of the day—the memories of the way Emily had looked coming down the aisle toward him, the kisses they had shared—everything good was buried now beneath the damning knowledge that he had gone about this whole thing the wrong way.

This house, these furnishings, everything he had done had only created a pretty shell in which to place his ready-made family, his half loaf that he had believed would make up for what he thought he would never have.

Now he had that family, and he had discovered a love more real than the one he had felt for Julia. A foundation on which he and Emily could build a wonderful life. Stupid and bumbling as he had been, he had somehow stumbled into paradise.

Yet everything was wrong. The pieces weren't falling neatly into place anymore.

The reality of what he had done, and the way in which he'd gone about doing it, descended on Luke like a dark cloud as the clock went on ticking, until he fell asleep sitting on the couch, waiting for his bride who slept with her daughter, the ice cubes melting in his glass.

Even as he slept his thoughts repeated in his head, like a record stuck forever in a single groove.

Too late.

Too soon.

Backward.

Chapter Nine

SCORPIO: Not a power day. Review, retrench, approach problems, seek solutions from another angle. Focus on continued domestic adjustments. There's safety in numbers. Evening brings enlightenment, shows the way to happiness.

Morning sunlight poured through the lacy white curtains of the large bay window in the kitchen as Sarah and Michael squirmed in their chairs, waiting for the first batch of blueberry pancakes to finish bubbling on the built-in griddle of the island stove.

Luke poured freshly squeezed orange juice into glasses, then moved to the old, dented coffeepot, planning to get himself a second cup of freshly brewed liquid. Emily had insisted upon bringing the old pot to the new house, vowing that no computerized machine could brew anything to compare to the coffee made in a well-loved pot.

He brushed past Emily, who was dressed in kelly green slacks and a pristine white blouse, her hair still damp from her morning shower. She and the children had come downstairs bright and early, waking him as one of them had led Fred in from the garage and the dog had bounded onto the couch to lick Luke's face.

But, other than to ask him what he wanted for breakfast, barely had a dozen excruciatingly polite words passed between him and Emily since he had come downstairs from his own shower.

In short, they looked and sounded like any other family—any other family, that is, in which the parents weren't speaking to each other. The tension in the air was so thick Luke wondered why he couldn't see it, smell it, taste it. But all he could smell was freshly brewed coffee and blueberry pancakes.

"Luke?"

"Yes, Michael?" Luke responded absently, sneaking a look at the growing pile of pancakes as he sniffed another aroma, that of frying bacon, his mouth beginning to water in anticipation of the coming feast. As honeymoon breakfasts went, this one was shaping up to be delicious—if slightly crowded.

"Michael!" Emily exclaimed, pointing the pancake turner in her son's direction. "Who gave you permission to call Dr. Manning 'Luke'?"

"I guess I did, Emily," Luke inserted quickly, not wanting Michael to tell his mother about their late-night conversation. "Do you mind?"

He would have given a great deal to know what Emily was thinking as he watched a myriad emotions flit across her face. "No," she said at last, dragging out the word. "I suppose not. If you don't, that is."

Luke grinned, relaxing. "It beats having them call me Dr. Manning," he said truthfully. "It's not like we had a lot to choose from, you know. And 'hey, you!' was out of the question."

"You've got a point." Emily laughed and handed him a plate stacked with pancakes, asking him to put it on the table. It was strange, Luke realized with a small start. They worked together as if they had been preparing family breakfasts for years. They seemed to anticipate what the other needed, what the other wanted, and divided up the care of the children so everything went smoothly.

"Luke," Michael called again, so that Luke realized the boy had been trying to engage him in conversation. "Mister Rafferty told me a joke yesterday. Do you want to hear it?"

"Go for it, tiger," Luke said, glad to see Emily happy again. After all, it couldn't have been any easier for her to awaken this morning beside her daughter than it had been for him to fall asleep on the couch last night.

"Okay," Michael said. "Here goes. Do you know how never to get bitten by a shark?"

Luke pulled out a chair for Emily as she came to the table, a platter of still-sizzling bacon in her hand. "No, tiger, I guess I don't. How do you never get bitten by a shark?"

"You don't ever leave Kansas!" Michael pronounced gleefully, turning from Luke to his mother as if eager to see their reaction to the joke. They laughed, obliging him.

"That's dumb. What's a Kansas?" Sarah asked, licking syrup from her fingers as Emily snatched the plastic bottle out of the child's other hand before it fell to the floor.

"I don't know, Sarah," Michael answered, pulling a face at his sister. "It's just a joke. Isn't it, Luke?"

It took most of the time spent at breakfast to explain the geographical joke to Sarah's satisfaction—not even attempting to point out its deeper meaning, that of allowing fear to keep a person from ever taking a chance—and she left the table still proclaiming that the joke was "dopey."

As Luke lingered over his third cup of coffee, wondering how to apologize to Emily for making such a mess of their wedding night, the children finally went outside to play with Fred. Much as he had wished to be alone with his new wife, he felt strangely defenseless now that the children had gone. How could he begin? And where?

"I'm sorry I fell asleep," Emily said, beating him to the punch. "It's just that yesterday was such a long day—finishing my last-minute packing, bathing the children and getting them ready, getting myself ready, making sure the flowers got to the chapel—all sorts of things. I—I guess I didn't realize how tired I was until I lay down."

She picked up two plates and walked toward the sink. "Is your neck feeling any better? I saw you rubbing at it earlier. I guess the couch isn't *that* comfortable.''

"I deserve a stiff neck," Luke answered, joining her at the sink, two more syrup-sticky dishes in his hands. "Actually, I deserve a good swift kick in the pants. I don't know why I caved in like that when Sarah started to cry. I guess I didn't want to be labeled the 'wicked stepfather.' Maybe I just want her to like me."

Emily began rinsing the dishes and stacking them in the dishwasher. "I would have warned you what Sarah was up to, but it's probably better that you figured it out for yourself. But she does like you, Luke. As a matter of fact, Sarah adores you. It's just that she's had me to herself all these years, especially these last couple of weeks, and I suppose she sees you as a threat. This whole marriage business has been quite an adjustment for her. But please don't let her walk all over you. We just have to give her some time to get used to us as a family."

Luke walked back to the table and returned with a handful of glasses. "Time," he repeated, handing them to Emily. "That's not a bad idea—for all of us. I think we might all need a little more time to become adjusted to all the changes our marriage and moving to a new home entails. Or is it only me that feels we've been stuck in fast-forward for the past month or more?"

"There may have been a few skid marks on the aisle runner yesterday at the chapel," Emily agreed, her smile telling him that she was willing to see the humor in their current situation. "All right, Luke," she continued, her smile expanding into a grin. "I forgive you."

"Oh, you do, do you? Our first fight, and I've lost," Luke quipped, relaxing his guard as he slung a dish towel over his left shoulder. "I hope this isn't an omen."

"Oh, I don't know," Emily remarked, taking the dish towel and hanging it on the rack inside the cabinet under the sink. "I kinda like it, myself."

"You would," Luke said, openly admiring her trim figure as she straightened once more and removed her apron. He leaned against the countertop, looking around the kitchen and its adjoining family room. *Family room. A room designed for families. Yet he had slept there last night, alone.*

"But you're right about the pace we've set ourselves, Emily, and it's time we installed a few speed bumps. Mrs. Manning," he said a moment later, coming to a decision, "I do believe today is Sunday. Thanks to extreme foresight on my part, and the fact that a certain surgeon in town owed me a big favor, I am not on call again until Tuesday morning. In other words, we have nothing to do all day today and tomorrow but get to know each other better—all of us."

Emily smiled in what looked to be real pleasure—and relief? "That sounds lovely, Dr. Manning, and it's the best wedding present yet. Shall we start with a tour of your new home? Excuse me—*our* new home. You haven't had time to be here much, and I've made some changes in a few of the rooms. I—I'd really like you to see them. And I planted some flowers in the backyard, along the base of the deck."

Her soft brown eyes were suddenly lit with enthusiasm and pride. He knew she had been working hard, and he did look forward to seeing what she had done.

"Planted flowers? When did you have the time? Never mind, I'm just glad that you feel at home here."

"How could I feel otherwise?" she asked, closing the dishwasher and heading for the French doors in the family room. "My husband and children live here. Oh, and by the way, *husband*, the grass needs to be cut."

It took everything he had in him to keep from racing after Emily, pulling her into his arms and kissing her until her toes tingled, but, somehow, he managed it. Instead, Luke pushed himself away from the counter and followed her outside to look at the flowers, not that he knew a daisy from a doorknob.

Retrench. Regroup. Go back to go forward. Do it slow and easy this time, Manning, he told himself, *and you might get it right yet!*

They each bathed one of the children that evening, Emily treating Sarah to a bubble bath in the "big" tub, while Luke introduced Michael to the shower in the family bathroom. Afterward, eating popcorn Emily had prepared in the hot-air popcorn maker that had been a wedding present from an internist at the hospital—complete with a note about how cholesterol-free popcorn was healthier—they all sat in the family room watching television.

Sarah, much to Luke's delight, crawled onto his lap halfway through the show, yawning widely as she laid her head against his chest. He didn't know which thrilled him more, the fact that she seemed to like him again, or the knowledge that the child was sleepy.

He sneaked a look at his wristwatch. Almost bedtime.

They'd had a good day, especially the hour they had spent unwrapping the remainder of the presents that had been delivered to the house in the last hectic days before the wedding. Emily had laughed as she extracted a toaster from a box at the same time Luke removed its exact twin from the box at his feet.

"Doctors don't seem to have much imagination, do they?" he had asked a few minutes later when Emily held up yet a third toaster.

Emily hadn't answered. She had just sat propped against the base of the living-room couch, shaking her head slowly as she held out a large white card. "Here, Luke, read this."

The card had been from Julia and Max, and inside was a confirmed reservation for two for the weekend of their choice at a large, luxury Manhattan hotel. Julia had signed their names to the card and, underneath, Max had added in his bold, flamboyant script, "And take Emily to a show while you're there—if you can find your way out of the room!"

As he had finished reading the card he had looked at Emily and took heart when he saw that for once she wasn't blushing. She was simply smiling, a slow, dreamy smile. "New York City. You know, Luke, I've never been to New York, which is ridiculous, as it's only a few hours away. We can go, can't we?"

"We can," he had answered, "as long as you promise not to write our thank-you note to Max until we get back. Otherwise, he might just show up on our doorstep with a trio of violin players to serenade us.''

Later, after touring every room of the house, some of them only for the second time, and discussing his plans for a small home office in the rooms to the rear of the garage, Luke had ordered a pizza for dinner over Emily's protests that she didn't mind cooking for them.

And now they were in the family room, watching television, two well-scrubbed, pajama-clad children yawning their way toward bedtime.

"Well, that's it," Emily said, rising as she employed the remote control to switch off the television set, then turning to hold out a hand to Michael to help him off the couch. "Eight-thirty and time for bed. Come on, kids, let's hit the toothbrushes."

Luke carried Sarah up the stairs, his manly feelings of possession swelling with each step he took, looking back down the stairs when he reached the upstairs hallway. Michael's discarded sneakers sat just beside the impressive double front doors, and Sarah had left a doll on top of the mahogany side table. This house may have been a cleverly decorated model a few weeks ago, but it was a home now—smelling of fresh flowers, clean children and warm popcorn.

Together, Emily and Luke tucked the children into their beds, activated the intercoms, then retraced their steps to the family room. "Would you like a glass of wine?" he asked, already heading for the bar. *Go slow,* he reminded himself. *Yes, you're alone now. Yes, she's incredibly lovely and you want to kiss her, hold her, make mad, passionate love to her. But not yet.*

Emily smiled her agreement as she sat on one of the couches, tucking her feet up on the cushion beside her. "I don't think we'll have any trouble from Sarah tonight. That walk we took around the neighborhood before dinner really tired her out. Good suggestion."

"Yes, I know. I'm a genius," Luke answered, handing her a long-stemmed glass filled with her favorite white wine. "Now if Michael doesn't decide it's his turn to have nightmares, maybe we can enjoy the evening."

Emily took a sip of wine, then placed the glass beside her on the end table. "Luke—about Michael," she began, her tone serious. "I don't think I approve of him calling you by your first name. It seems, well, disrespectful. After all, you're his stepfather now, not his new friend."

Luke sat beside her, his drink left on the bar, untouched. "What would you suggest, Emily? He can't keep calling me Dr. Manning. When he asked me my opinion, I left the choice up to him. He picked 'Luke.'"

"And you're happy with that?" she asked, looking up at him, her light brown eyes the exact shade of her son's. Sarah's eyes were blue, most probably an inheritance from her father. If they had a child together, he and Emily, would that child have those same warm brown eyes, or would they be coal dark, like his?

Luke stood, carefully putting some distance between himself and temptation. "Happy?" He turned away. "No, Emily, it doesn't make me happy. I'd be lying if I told you it makes me happy that Michael calls me Luke. Sarah doesn't call me anything—did you notice that? I'll be helping you to raise Michael and Sarah, until they finish college. I had hoped for more than 'Luke.' Maybe it will come, in time."

He heard the soft rustle of her linen slacks as she stood and walked over to him to rest her head against his back. "Michael called Mark 'Daddy,' although I doubt he remembers it," she said quietly. "I've always kept pictures of Mark in their rooms, but Michael was so young—I don't think he remembers him anymore. And Sarah never knew him at all."

Luke turned, taking hold of her shoulders. "But you do, Emily. You remember Mark. Tell me about him, please."

She avoided his gaze, and when she spoke, her tone was bitter, surprising him with its vehemence. "There's really nothing to talk about. He was a fireman. He died a hero. I have the medals to prove it."

"And you're mad at him for dying, aren't you, Emily?" Luke asked, suddenly sure he was right. Emily didn't talk about her late husband because she resented him for dying, for being a dead hero. What Emily needed, what she wanted, then and now, was a live husband.

She pulled away, picking up her wineglass, although she didn't take a drink. "I thought we were going to talk, Luke, get to know each other better, the way we should have done before we went through with this marriage. You didn't tell me you were going to launch an inquisition."

Now Luke returned to the bar, because he needed to take a drink of the wine he had poured. It tasted bitter on his tongue. "But I'm right, aren't I? You know, it's funny. I couldn't keep Julia because Max was always in the background. I thought I had the same problem with Mark—competing with your love for him. Of course, I also thought we could have a good marriage, based on friendship—friendship that might someday grow into affection. That's all I wanted, or so I thought.

"I believed passion was over for me, that I didn't want it again. But I was wrong, Emily. I do want the passion. You're my wife now. I want to love you. I want you to love me. Julia and I have become friends, settling the past. But you aren't finished with Mark yet. You aren't ready for another love."

Emily collapsed onto the couch, her warm brown eyes suddenly, uncharacteristically cold and flashing with anger. It was as if she had not heard him mention the word *love* in relationship to the two of them. "Why, Dr. Manning, you are a man of many talents. Why didn't you tell me you minored in psychology? But you're wrong, Doctor. It's not Mark I have trouble forgiving."

"Emily—"

"No!" She held out a hand, cutting him off. "No, Luke, let me speak, please. Let me tell you about Mark. Let me tell you all about Mark. All about me. I should have told you at the very beginning. After all, you were honest with me about Julia. Now it's my turn."

Suddenly Luke didn't want to know about Emily's first husband. He didn't want to know how they'd met or how they had fallen in love or when they had married—or what their life together had been like.

But he had opened this particular can of worms, and Emily didn't appear ready to back off now. "Mark and I dated exclusively since junior high school. I never dated anyone except Mark, terrible as that sounds. When Sarah is old enough I want her to date dozens of boys. I want her to experience more of life, of different people, before she marries."

She shook her head as if clearing it. "But that's in the future. Let's get back to Mark. When I was in my senior year, and Mark was a sophomore in college, my mother died. My dad had died years earlier. Mark's father took me in. After that, there was no question of dating anyone else. Mark and I were married exactly a year after I graduated."

She kept her head down as she talked, turning the engagement ring Luke had given her round and round her finger. "It was wonderful, being married. At least, it was at first. We lived in a small apartment just off campus, and I had to go to the laundromat to do our wash. Mark refused to let me go alone. He said men would look at me. I was flattered, especially since I was pregnant with Michael at the time.

"But soon Mark wouldn't let me go to the supermarket alone, either, for the same reason. And if I didn't answer the phone when he called me from work—he quit college in his last year to follow his father into the fire department—he'd question me about where I had been. Usually I was taking Michael for a walk or talking to a neighbor. Mark would go to that neighbor and ask if I had really been talking with her.

I sometimes think he joined the fire department so that we could move in with his father and he could work different shifts each week, keep unpredictable hours—the better to check up on me.''

Luke stood very still, listening to Emily's every word. He tried to imagine Emily coping with such unreasonable jealousy, but he couldn't. The picture of Emily as a totally submissive, even cowed woman was impossible to conjure. But she had been very young and alone in the world except for Mark and his father. What else could she have done?

''It got so that I was afraid to go out of the house, embarrassed by Mark's displays of jealousy, his wild temper tantrums. When—when I didn't want to make love, when I was tired from being with Michael all day long, Mark would accuse me of meeting men in the afternoon, while he and his father were at work and Michael slept. He was even jealous of Michael, of the time I spent with him.''

She looked up at Luke, her eyes awash with unshed tears. ''I wasn't married to Mark, Luke. I was never really married to Mark. I was his possession. At the end I don't think I could remember a time when I loved him. I do know I didn't like him. The day—the day he died, the same day I learned that I was pregnant with Sarah, I had decided to leave him. He hadn't wanted any more babies and I couldn't face another scene, even if Michael and I would have had to sleep on a park bench. I was packing Michael's clothes when the fire chief came to the door to tell me the news. It was almost as if I had wished Mark dead.''

Her hands stilled in her lap. "I stayed on with Mark's father, until he was killed on the job a year later, then lived in his house with Michael and Sarah until the upkeep became too much for me. You know the rest."

She looked at Luke, who had been silent, stunned by her admission, and he could see the tears that were now running freely down her cheeks. "And that's probably the biggest reason why I said yes to you, Luke. You didn't make me feel threatened. You wanted a family—not a possession. You couldn't possibly be jealous, because you weren't marrying me for love. We'd both benefit. It seemed a good trade-off."

Luke put down his glass and approached Emily carefully, so as not to frighten her. "And do you think that I've changed the rules? Do you think I want you as a possession now, Emily?"

She bit her lip and shook her head. "No. Unlike Mark, you know the difference between people and things. This house is a possession, and one to be proud of, but you know I'm a person. To tell you the truth, I did think you were using me as a substitute for Julia. Especially when I saw her name on the list of wedding guests. That made *me* jealous, an emotion I fought because I didn't want to be like Mark. But then I met her, and I knew I had been wrong."

She took a step in his direction. A single step but an important one, for both of them. "I'm nothing like Julia. I'm just a mother, a woman whose greatest ambition in life is to have a home and family, and I'm not ashamed of that fact. I'm proud of it. You may have loved Julia, Luke, but you need me. I think you do love me a little. And I think I love you. No—I *know* I love you. I didn't mean to, but I do. You're not a substitute for Mark. I love you, Luke, and I want to make a home with you, and I want my children to call you Daddy, and I want—''

Luke didn't let her finish. There was no reason for her to finish; he knew what she wanted. What they both wanted. Taking the last two steps that brought him in front of her, he gathered her into his arms.

Somehow, without really thinking about it, he maneuvered them over to the couch, still locked in each other's arms, her mouth warm and pliant beneath his and tasting of her tears. They subsided onto the soft cushions, side by side, their arms and legs entangled, their hands seeking to draw each other closer, ever closer as a burst of passion overtook them.

This would be their wedding night, their first night, the real beginning. Luke sensed it, felt it deep in his heart. His hand went to the top button of Emily's blouse; a surgeon's hands, strong and sure. But now they trembled, shook, so that his fingers fumbled, barely able to negotiate the small buttons that concealed what he longed to touch, to taste, to love and, yes, to *possess*.

Emily pushed herself back against the cushions, easing Luke's way, allowing him to rid her of the blouse, exposing the filmy lace that was his last barrier. He cupped her breasts through the thin material, feeling her blossom under his hands, then trailed his fingers to her waist, smoothing the lush contour of her hip as he pressed himself against her, a voice somewhere inside his head reminding him to go slow, to measure his advances.

He instinctively sensed that Emily had not been allowed to enjoy lovemaking with Mark, for jealous people were also selfish people, involved only with their own needs, their own pleasures. Although Emily had been a wife, although she was mother to two children, she was undoubtedly unfamiliar with the true glory to be found in *making* love with someone you loved.

He was glad he had taken the time to draw back, to move her forward slowly. He could feel her trembling as he moved his hand upward once more, shivering slightly as he slid his fingertips along the upper edge of lace, learning her by touch, the discovery of the small metal front closure nearly undermining his determination to let her set the pace.

She tasted so sweet. He could kiss her forever, just to taste that sweetness. But he needed more, and he prayed she was ready. He drew slightly away from her, then began trailing small kisses down her throat, across the creamy expanse above the lacy wisp.

If he had experienced passion before in his life, he couldn't remember it now.

He had nothing to compare with the feelings flowing through him, no reference to relate to the rush of love, of tenderness that filled him as she inserted a hand between them and moved to unlock the metal clasp, to offer him her body in sweet surrender, issuing a shuddering sigh somewhere above his ear.

And that's when he made the most difficult decision of his life, a decision he couldn't have made earlier, before he'd learned the truth about Emily's life with Mark.

That's when Luke pushed his passion back under control and laid his hand on hers, silently shaking his head. The evening, her admissions, had been too traumatic. It wouldn't be fair to make love to her now. "No, Emily. Not yet. We aren't ready for this yet. Much as we both want it. It's not time."

He pulled the edges of her blouse together, then bent to claim her lips once more, his kiss soft, gentle and no longer demanding, before he took her hand and helped her to her feet.

"Luke?" she questioned, eyeing him strangely.

He laughed, mostly at himself, at his stupid promise to take it slowly, not to rush her. "You asked to be courted, Mrs. Manning, and I promised to do just that. I'd like to think I keep my promises. We have the rest of our lives to be together, Emily, but we only have this time to fall in love. We've done everything else backward. Let's do this part right."

The confusion faded from her eyes, to be replaced by a shining look that would have had him congratulating himself for his brilliance if he didn't want her so much. Now. Not next week. Not ten minutes from now. But *now!*

"Luke, this is silly. We've just admitted that we love each other. They weren't entirely romantic admissions—I think I may have yelled mine—but all the same, we've made them. You don't have to give me romance. Not now. We're *married.* Oh, Luke—are you sure about this?"

"No, sweetheart," he admitted, "but I am determined. Come on, wife," he said, taking her hand. "It's time you were in bed."

"But, Luke," she protested. She took her time buttoning her blouse, perhaps even flirting with him as she did it, something he felt sure she wouldn't have done before he had told her that he wouldn't press her for anything more that night. "It's only a little after nine o'clock. I'll never be able to sleep."

He grinned, then guided her toward the foyer, his arm around her shoulders. "Neither will I, sweetheart. Neither will I. People who are falling in love aren't supposed to be able to sleep. Now let me walk you 'home.'"

They stopped in front of the door to her bedroom, to stand close together, staring into each other's eyes. "I guess this is good night, Emily," Luke said at last. "The end of our first, very short, date. Dream of me?"

She didn't speak, but only nodded, then went up on tiptoe to kiss his cheek. "Good night, Luke," she whispered, opening her door, to disappear behind it a moment later. The door opened again and she stuck her head out, smiling, to say, "I forgot to tell you. Thank you, Luke. I had a *very* nice time! Oh, and by the away—you're a crazy man. But I *do* love you!"

He stood there for about a minute—or maybe an hour—after she'd closed the door again, before turning down the hall to enter the master bedroom. The room was partially lit by the full moon that peeked in through the skylights over the bed. The bed he hadn't slept in last night.

Luke stood looking at the bed for a minute—or an hour—before grabbing a blanket and pillow from the dressing room and heading for the couch in the sitting alcove.

There was no way he was getting into that bed until Emily was there, lying between the sheets in the moonlight, waiting for him.

After all, it was their marriage bed.

It was nearing midnight when the door to the master suite opened and Emily stepped inside. Freshly bathed and dressed in her new peignoir, she tiptoed toward the bed, which was still illuminated in the moonlight.

Luke wasn't there. The decorative quilt hadn't been disturbed, all the many throw pillows still lay where she had put them when she had made up the bed with such care—and slightly trembling hands—the day before they were married.

Biting her bottom lip, she looked toward the dressing area and bathroom, but saw no light under the door.

Tears stung the back of her eyes as she turned to leave, planning to see if he had decided to sleep in the family room once more.

And then she saw him.

His long frame was bent uncomfortably in the small love seat, one hand dragging on the floor, the blanket lying low on his bare chest, exposing his lean, well-muscled body.

"Luke?" she questioned softly, going down onto her knees beside him. "Luke, wake up, please. What are you doing here?"

He instantly came awake, probably, she thought, due to the many times he had been awakened in the middle of the night to treat one of his patients. She watched as he jackknifed to a sitting position and ran a hand through his dark hair. "Emily? What is it? Is something wrong? Is one of the children sick?"

She shook her head, reaching out a hand to touch his bare chest, to thread her fingers through the dark mat of hair that so intrigued her. He placed his own hand on top of hers, his thumb rubbing against her palm. "The kids are fine, Luke," she said, hearing the tremor in her voice and recognizing it for what it was. Passion. Passion and a longing to love such as she had never felt before. "Honestly. But—but I couldn't sleep."

"You couldn't?" Luke questioned, his voice low as his hand left hers to travel to her chin, his long fingers tracing the soft curve from her ear to the sensitive corner of her mouth. "Why, Emily?"

Surely he already knew. He had to know. But he would wait for her to say it. That was one of the many reasons she loved him—why she would always love him.

"Luke," she said, straining to look into his eyes in the darkness. "I think you're wonderful to be so considerate of me. In fact, if you were any more considerate of me I might be prompted to choke you! But I've made a decision." She smiled now, feeling freer than she had in a long, long time. "Luke—I want to leave Kansas."

He was quiet for a moment, and then a soft chuckle issued from deep in his throat. "Me, too, my beautiful wife—my life," he said. "Me, too."

Luke scooped his wife into his arms and gently deposited her in the spill of moonlight that played across the bed.

"I love you, Emily Manning," he said, looking down at her as she held up her arms, freely inviting him into her arms, her life—completely and totally.

And then he joined her on the bed.

Epilogue

YOUR DAILY ASTROLOGICAL FORECAST

SCORPIO: A real firecracker of a day! Project be-gun months earlier comes to fruition. Be ready for excitement, possible addition to family.

"Emily! For God's sake, what do you think you're doing?"

Emily put down the long-handled brush and turned to look at her husband. "What does it look like I'm doing, Luke? I'm cleaning this tub. Michael must have brought half of the backyard inside with him. What were you three doing outside—planting a tree or dig-ging up some lost civilization?"

"Very funny," Luke retorted, looking at his wife as she sat on the platform leading to the oversize tub—a small pile of plastic toy boats beside her—her nine-months-pregnant body clad in a red, white and blue sundress in honor of the day. "I could have done that."

"I know you could have, darling, but I wanted to take a bath. At least, I did until I remembered that Ben said I should stick to showers until this baby is born. I don't know what's wrong with me, Luke. I've been so tired lately, yet today I'm full of energy. All I want to do is work. Luke, do you remember that night we brought glasses of wine upstairs and took turns bathing each other? Oh, how I miss those days. Sometimes I think I'll never fit in this tub again—especially since Michael and Sarah seem to consider it their private swimming pool."

"I remember, darling. As a matter of fact, if I recall correctly, that night was what got you in this condition." Then Luke considered everything Emily had said and looked at her closely, memories of his stint in obstetrics coming back to him. Women about to go into labor sometimes experienced an unusual burst of energy; something to do with wanting to exercise their nest-building instincts or something like that.

"Emily. Sweetheart?" he said carefully, measuring his words. "Maybe we ought to call Ben, just to make sure he's on call today."

"Don't be silly, Luke. And stop looking at me as if I'm going to burst at any moment. I'm not due for another—*oh!*"

Luke was beside her in an instant. "'Oh?' Oh, what, sweetheart? Did you feel something? What did you feel? Is it the baby? Emily?"

She smiled up at him, still unable to believe that a man like Luke, a doctor, could fall to pieces every time she so much as flinched. As she had already told him countless times, pregnant ladies flinched when the baby kicked, or when they moved too suddenly. Countless reasons.

"Luke, it was nothing. Just a little twinge—nothing to get excited about. Now, please, help me up. *Oh!*" She sat very still, her soft brown eyes wide, waiting for the contraction to pass. "Well, now," she commented as he helped pull her to her feet, "maybe that one *was* more than just a twinge. Oh, dear—and I have an apple pie in the oven, too."

Luke supported her at the elbow as he ushered her back into the bedroom and made her sit on the love seat. "A pie? Lady, that's not all you have 'in the oven,' as the locals say. Now stay right here—I'm calling Ben."

"Yes, darling," Emily answered obediently, although her eyes were twinkling. "Besides, I love it when you're being masterful. *Oh!*"

Luke pushed a hand through his hair again, beginning to look very much unstrung. "That does it! You told me you delivered Sarah in three hours, for crying out loud! I'm calling Madge to have her pick up the kids. We're going to the hospital!"

"Luke, you're standing in front of it again. How am I supposed to concentrate on my 'focal point' if you keep getting in the way?"

Luke quickly stepped to one side so that Emily could look at the small replica of the Statue of Liberty, a memento from their honeymoon weekend in New York City. "Sorry, sweetheart," he said, feeling as clumsy and as out of place as Fred would be in a china shop.

And as useless. After helping Emily into bed in the prettily decorated "birthing room," he had changed into greens, with every intention of assisting in the birth of his child.

Only it wasn't working out that way. As a matter of fact, only ten minutes ago Ben Easterly had threatened to have him bodily removed from the room. Luke had been unable to do much more than hold Emily's hand, wipe her forehead with a cool cloth, and ask questions.

Boy, he thought, wincing, did he ask questions. At last even Emily, bless her, had hinted that he might be of more use in the waiting room, sitting with Michael, Sarah and Madge.

Didn't they understand? This was his *wife* lying here! His wife, in pain! God, how did other men stand this? And she was being so brave; much braver than he. She was the axis of his world, his universe, the calm center of any storm life might send to him. What if something went wrong? What if he lost her? God! He couldn't imagine a life without Emily, without this woman he loved with every fiber of his being.

"Emily? How do you feel?" Ben asked, taking up his position at the bottom of the bed. "Do you think you could push again? Good. You're doing great, Emily. Really great. Best patient I ever had—which is a helluva lot more than I can say for your husband."

"Put a sock in it, Ben," Luke grumbled, knowing the other man was right.

Ben ignored him. "Now, Emily, when the next contraction comes, I'd like you to push again, just one more time. That ought to do it. Luke? You want to play catcher?"

It was coming. The baby was coming. Dear God, his baby was coming! Luke looked at the obstetrician as if the man had asked him to put on a uniform and play for the Yankees. "What?"

"Emily, how do you put up with this guy? *Catcher*, Luke," Ben repeated, smiling and shaking his head. "Get a grip, man. I asked if you would like to deliver your baby. And you'd better make up your mind in a hurry, because this kid isn't going to wait much longer."

Five minutes later Luke held his new daughter in his arms, tears streaming down his face as he looked at the small scrap of humanity, the miracle he and Emily had created through their love.

He had not only delivered his own child, but Ben had let him cut the cord, making everything official. The lustily crying Susan Michele Manning had become the new addition to their family. Their new daughter; their third child.

Luke touched one reverent finger to the infant's infinitesimally small hand, and immediately she clasped that finger in a strong grip, as if she already knew that he was her father. Her little hand might only be touching his fingertip, but he could feel those perfect fingers bonding tightly around his heart, squeezing it into an agony of bliss. A rush of complete and unconditional love swept over him, instantly pledging him to her for a lifetime and beyond.

Luke was stunned, in absolute awe, completely overwhelmed. He opened his mouth to speak, to say something—anything—but no words would come.

"Luke?" Emily questioned teasingly, although he heard the slight fatigue in her voice. Ben had been right: Emily had been splendid, and she had been "splendid" in something less than two hours. So why did he feel as if they'd been in this room for a month? "May I hold her now, please, or aren't you willing to give her up yet?"

"Nurse," Ben said, motioning for the smiling young woman in attendance to follow him out of the room. "Let's leave these three alone for a few minutes, all right? Luke, we'll let Michael and Sarah in soon, okay?"

Luke only nodded, for he was busy handing the tightly blanketed baby to Emily.

"Oh, Luke," Emily said as he kissed her forehead, longing to sweep her into his arms but knowing she had just been through an ordeal, no matter how wonderful she had been. "Susan looks just like you. And she has so much hair—so much lovely black hair. It must be three inches long. I never saw a newborn with so much hair."

Luke sat on the edge of the bed, still unashamedly wiping at the tears that didn't seem to stop flowing. "No, darling. Susan looks like you."

The infant closed her slate-blue eyes and yawned widely, instantly falling asleep. "Actually, Luke," Emily quipped, touching his tear-wet cheek, "with all this hair, she reminds me a lot of Fred. Oh, Luke, isn't she beautiful?''

Luke kissed her again. "Almost as beautiful as her mother,'' he said, his voice husky. "God, Emily, but I love you!''

Ben stuck his head into the room and cleared his throat. "Excuse me, guys, but Luke—you've got a telephone call. It's not an emergency, but the guy was pretty insistent. Says his name is Max. They'll put it through from the nurses' station.''

"Max?'' Luke questioned a moment later, speaking into the receiver. "How did you—what?'' He listened for some moments, smiling, and then said, "Susan Michele—one *L*—and Max, thanks.''

He replaced the receiver and turned back to Emily. "That was Max.''

"Yes, I had rather suspected it was,'' Emily answered, tucking the baby closer to her breast. "What I don't know is how he got the call put through in here. No, never mind. I do know how. Nobody could deny Max Rafferty anything. The real question is, why did he call?''

Luke sat on the edge of the bed once more and explained. "He read my horoscope for today and said there was something in it about Susan. When he called the house and no one answered, he immediately telephoned the hospital.''

"What?'' Emily was obviously confused.

"Don't ask, darling,'' Luke told her. "It's a long story. Just get ready to accept a package containing a silver engraved something-or-other. Ah—here come the kids!''

Michael and Sarah tiptoed into the room, looking around as if they might be caught and sent out again. But then Susan began to cry and all their inhibitions fled in their eagerness to see their new sister.

Luke picked up Sarah, gave her a hug and held her next to the bed. "There she is, kitten. What do you think?''

"Oh, Daddy, she looks just like one of my dolls!'' Sarah exclaimed. "Are we really going to be able to keep her?''

"Forever and ever, darling,'' Emily answered. "Even when she grows up a little and starts getting into your toys.''

Michael stood beside Luke, craning his neck to see. "Dad, is she supposed to be that little?'' he asked, reaching out a hand to touch one small foot that had somehow escaped the blanket. "Gee, another girl. She's cute and all, but I really kinda wanted a brother.''

Luke and Emily laughed, having already heard Michael's sentiments on the possibility the baby would be a girl. "Maybe next time, tiger, okay?'' Emily offered, smiling at their son.

"Keen!'' Michael turned to Luke. "When, Dad. When?''

"Oh, Michael!'' Luke and Emily exclaimed in unison as the nurse reentered the room, planning to take the baby out to be weighed and measured.

But when she looked at the family standing so close together: from the drowsy mother happily snuggling her infant; to the proud, handsome father holding that sweet little blond-haired angel high against his chest; to the freckle-faced boy with the untied sneakers who was gently fondling his new sister's toes.... Well, she decided, feeling misty-eyed herself as she quietly closed the door, some moments just shouldn't be disturbed.

* * * * *

LOVE AND
LOVE AND THE SCORPIO MAN

by Wendy Corsi Staub

Baby, it's cold outside! When November arrives with its brisk air and harsh weather, the sexy Scorpio man is ready to turn his thoughts to indoor activities— namely, romance! This attentive, passionate fellow just adores those stormy nights when the wind is howling outside, while inside, the right woman is snuggled beside him. After all, sharing body heat is his ideal method for staying warm!

In PRENUPTIAL AGREEMENT, Scorpio man Luke Manning has met his match in domestic Cancer woman Emily Cornell. There's no question that home, sweet home—with a pot of homemade stew and a blazing fire—is where these two can be found on cold November nights!

How would the Scorpio man warm your heart when a chill is in the air?

The *Aries* woman thrives on challenge, and she'll be fired up when the Scorpio man suggests a cozy evening at home enjoying their favorite board games.

While they're playing against each other, ultra-competitive Aries female will see her handsome mate as the enemy...but as soon as the games are over, she'll be willing to fraternize!

The Scorpio man knows the *Taurus* woman truly appreciates thoughtful little gifts to let her know he's thinking of her. She'll be positively charmed by an adorable stuffed teddy bear! She's sure to snuggle up with her furry new friend...*and* her real live sweetheart!

The *Gemini* woman *loves* to read, and while she enjoys the mental stimulation of nonfiction, sometimes she craves pure pleasure. She'll be perfectly content when the Scorpio man shows up with the latest bestselling romance novel...and slyiy suggests they act out her favorite scenes later!

The sun-worshiping *Leo* woman is out of sorts when the days turn gray and dreary, but the Scorpio man has just the thing to cheer her up and bring back that summer feeling: an indoor picnic! He'll spread a red-checked tablecloth on the carpet and spread out a feast fit for the Fourth of July: fried chicken, potato salad, deviled eggs and lemonade!

Though the holidays are still a month away, the super-organized *Virgo* woman is always a few steps ahead of everyone else. She'll appreciate the Scorpio man's offer to help her address her Christmas cards and wrap presents—but he won't be allowed to peek at his own gift, which is safely hidden away!

The Scorpio man has just the thing to keep the lovely *Libra* woman toasty...*and* fashionable! She'll be thrilled with the luxurious handmade cashmere sweater he's bought her—in the perfect colors for her sign: blue and lavender!

When *two Scorpios* get together, there's no question about where they can be found on a wintry night: in their big, cozy double bed! Piles of blankets and quilts will go a long way toward keeping them warm—and so will passion's flames.

The spontaneous *Sagittarius* woman can't sit still for long; she's always raring to go, and she won't be stopped by a little detail like the weather! If it's blustery and snowing, that's all the better—she'll drag the Scorpio man outside for a snowball fight, and before long it'll be a real party when all the neighbors join in!

The workaholic *Capricorn* woman often stays late at the office, but when she arrives home, she'll find that the Scorpio man knows just how to soothe her stressed-out nerves. Soft music is playing, the fire is roaring, and two steaming mugs of real hot cocoa—complete with whipped cream—are waiting to be savored.

The altruistic *Aquarius* woman is always concerned for those less fortunate when the temperatures plunge, and the Scorpio man admires her selflessness. Together, they'll bring blankets and coats to local homeless shelters and find that helping others is its own reward.

The dreamy *Pisces* woman loves nothing better than to get lost in a romantic fantasy, and the Scorpio man knows how to indulge her. He'll rent several classic love stories on video, pop a big bowl of popcorn and get cozy with his own leading lady on the couch for an evening of heartwarming viewing.

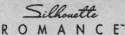

Silhouette
R O M A N C E™

HEARTLAND HOLIDAYS

Christmas bells turn into wedding bells for the Gallagher siblings in Stella Bagwell's *Heartland Holidays* trilogy.

THEIR FIRST THANKSGIVING (#903) in November
Olivia Westcott had once rejected Sam Gallagher's proposal—and in his stubborn pride, he'd refused to hear her reasons why. Now Olivia is back...and it is about time Sam Gallagher listened!

THE BEST CHRISTMAS EVER (#909) in December
Soldier Nick Gallagher had come home to be the best man at his brother's wedding—not to be a groom! But when he met single mother Allison Lee, he knew he'd found his bride.

NEW YEAR'S BABY (#915) in January
Kathleen Gallagher had given up on love and marriage until she came to the rescue of neighbor Ross Douglas...and the newborn baby he'd found on his doorstep!

Come celebrate the holidays with Silhouette Romance!

Take 4 bestselling love stories FREE

Plus get a FREE surprise gift!

Silhouette
Christmas
Stories
1992

Experience the beauty of Yuletide romance with Silhouette
Christmas Stories 1992—a collection of heartwarming stories by
favorite Silhouette authors.

JONI'S MAGIC by Mary Lynn Baxter
HEARTS OF HOPE by Sondra Stanford
THE NIGHT SANTA CLAUS RETURNED by Marie Ferrarrella
BASKET OF LOVE by Jeanne Stephens

Also available this year are three popular early editions of
Silhouette Christmas Stories—1986, 1987 and 1988. Look for
these and you'll be well on your way to a complete collection
of the best in holiday romance.

Plus, as an added bonus, you can receive a FREE keepsake
Christmas ornament. Just collect four proofs of purchase from
any November or December 1992 Harlequin or Silhouette series
novels, or from any Harlequin or Silhouette Christmas
collection, and receive a beautiful dated brass Christmas
candle ornament.

Mail this certificate along with four (4) proof-of-purchase coupons, plus $1.50 postage and
handling (check or money order—do not send cash), payable to Silhouette Books, to: **In the
U.S.:** P.O. Box 9057, Buffalo, NY 14269-9057; **In Canada:** P.O. Box 622, Fort Erie, Ontario,
L2A 5X3.